THE GIRL WHO OWNED A CITY

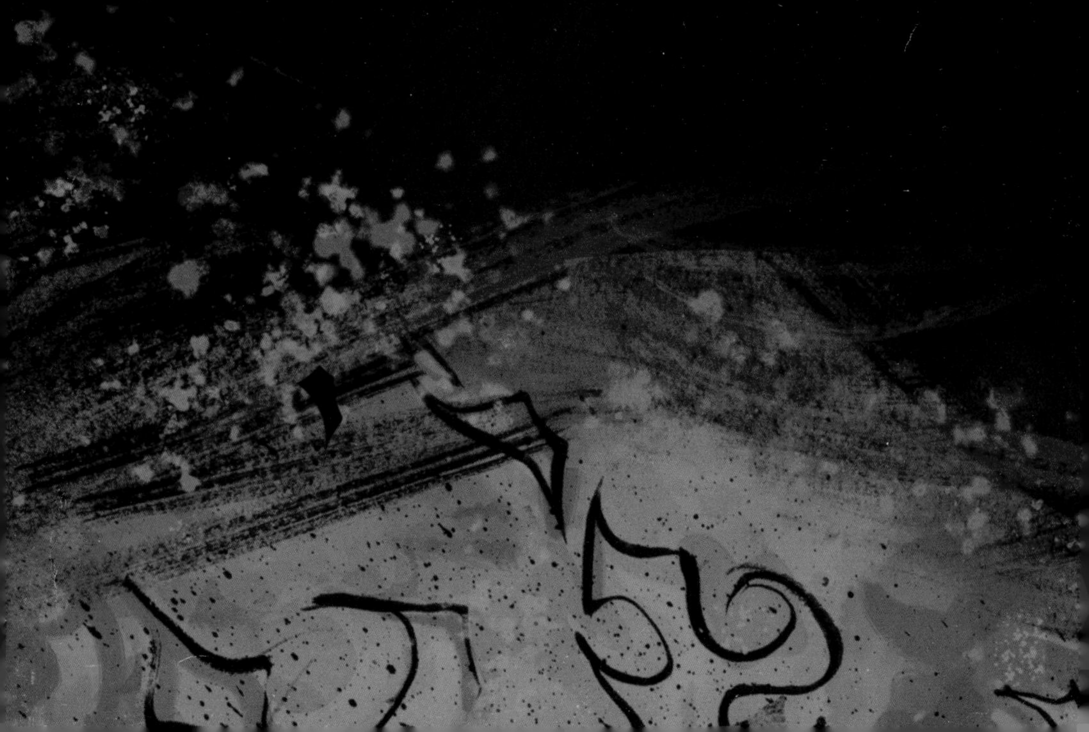

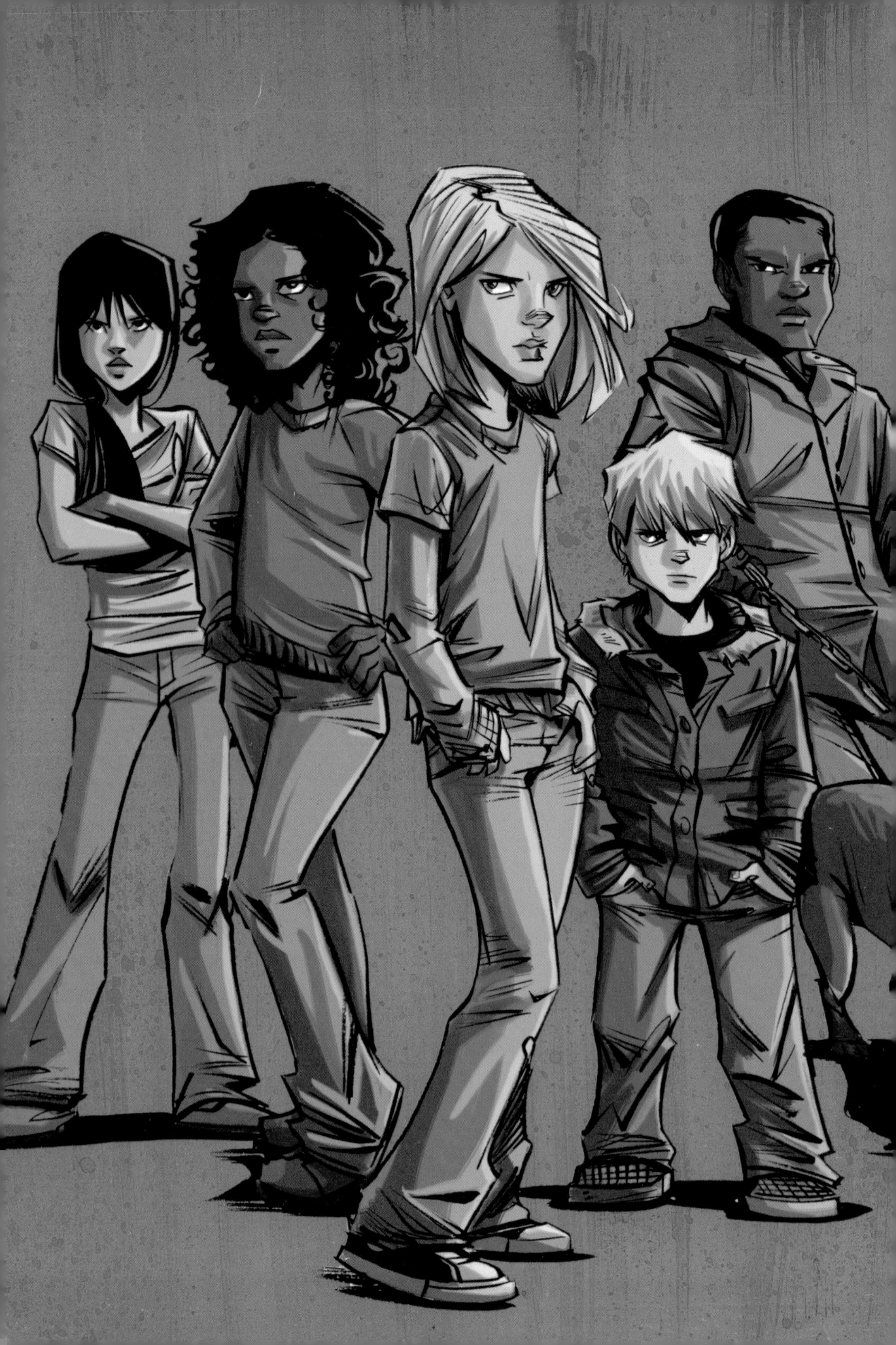

THE GIRL WHO OWNED A CITY

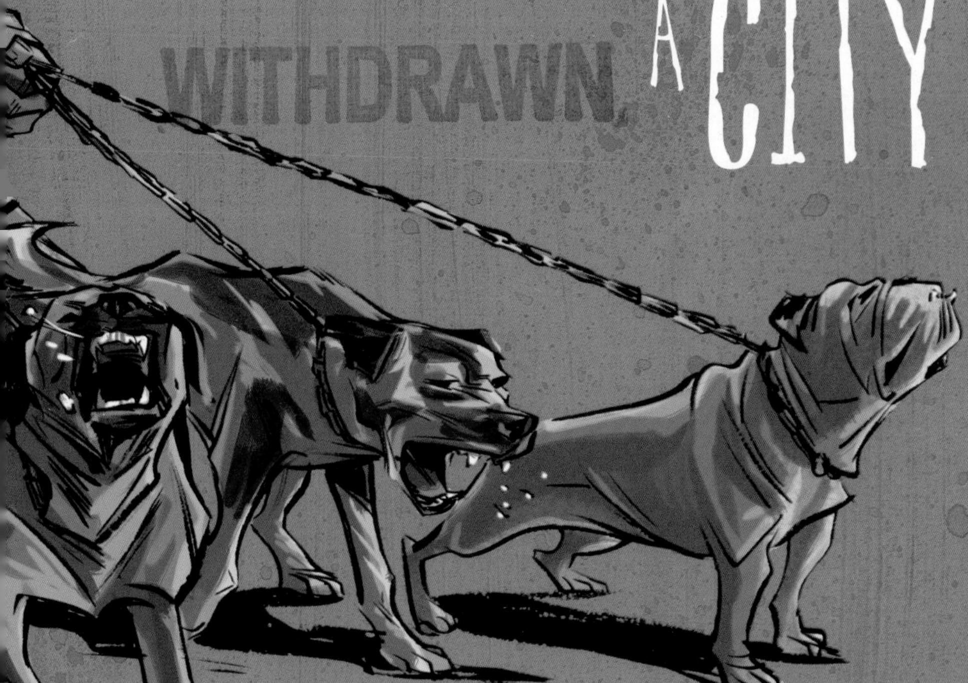

By O. T. NELSON • Adapted by DAN JOLLEY
Illustrated by JOËLLE JONES
Coloring by JENN MANLEY LEE

GRAPHIC UNIVERSE™ • MINNEAPOLIS • NEW YORK

FOR LISA AND TODD
—O. T. NELSON

STORY BY O. T. NELSON
ADAPTED BY DAN JOLLEY
PENCILS AND INKS BY JOËLLE JONES
COLORING BY JENN MANLEY LEE
LETTERING BY GRACE LU

GRAPHIC UNIVERSE™
A DIVISION OF LERNER PUBLISHING GROUP, INC.
241 FIRST AVENUE NORTH
MINNEAPOLIS, MN 55401 U.S.A.

WEBSITE ADDRESS: WWW.LERNERBOOKS.COM

MAIN BODY TEXT SET IN MEANWHILE.
TYPEFACE PROVIDED BY COMICRAFT/ACTIVE IMAGES.

LIBRARY OF CONGRESS CATALOGING-IN-PUBLICATION DATA

JOLLEY, DAN.
    THE GIRL WHO OWNED A CITY : THE GRAPHIC NOVEL / BY O. T. NELSON ; ADAPTED BY DAN
JOLLEY ; ILLUSTRATED BY JOËLLE JONES.
      P.   CM.
    SUMMARY: WHEN A PLAGUE SWEEPS OVER THE EARTH KILLING EVERYONE EXCEPT CHILDREN
UNDER TWELVE, LISA NELSON ORGANIZES A GROUP TO REBUILD A NEW WAY OF LIFE.
    ISBN: 978-0-7613-4903-7 (LIB. BDG. : ALK. PAPER)
    1. GRAPHIC NOVELS. [1. GRAPHIC NOVELS. 2. SURVIVAL—FICTION. 3. SCIENCE FICTION.]
I. JONES, JOËLLE, ILL. II. NELSON, O. T. GIRL WHO OWNED A CITY. III. TITLE.
PZ7.7.J6561 2012
741.5'973—DC22   2009033270

MANUFACTURED IN THE UNITED STATES OF AMERICA
1 – BP – 12/31/11

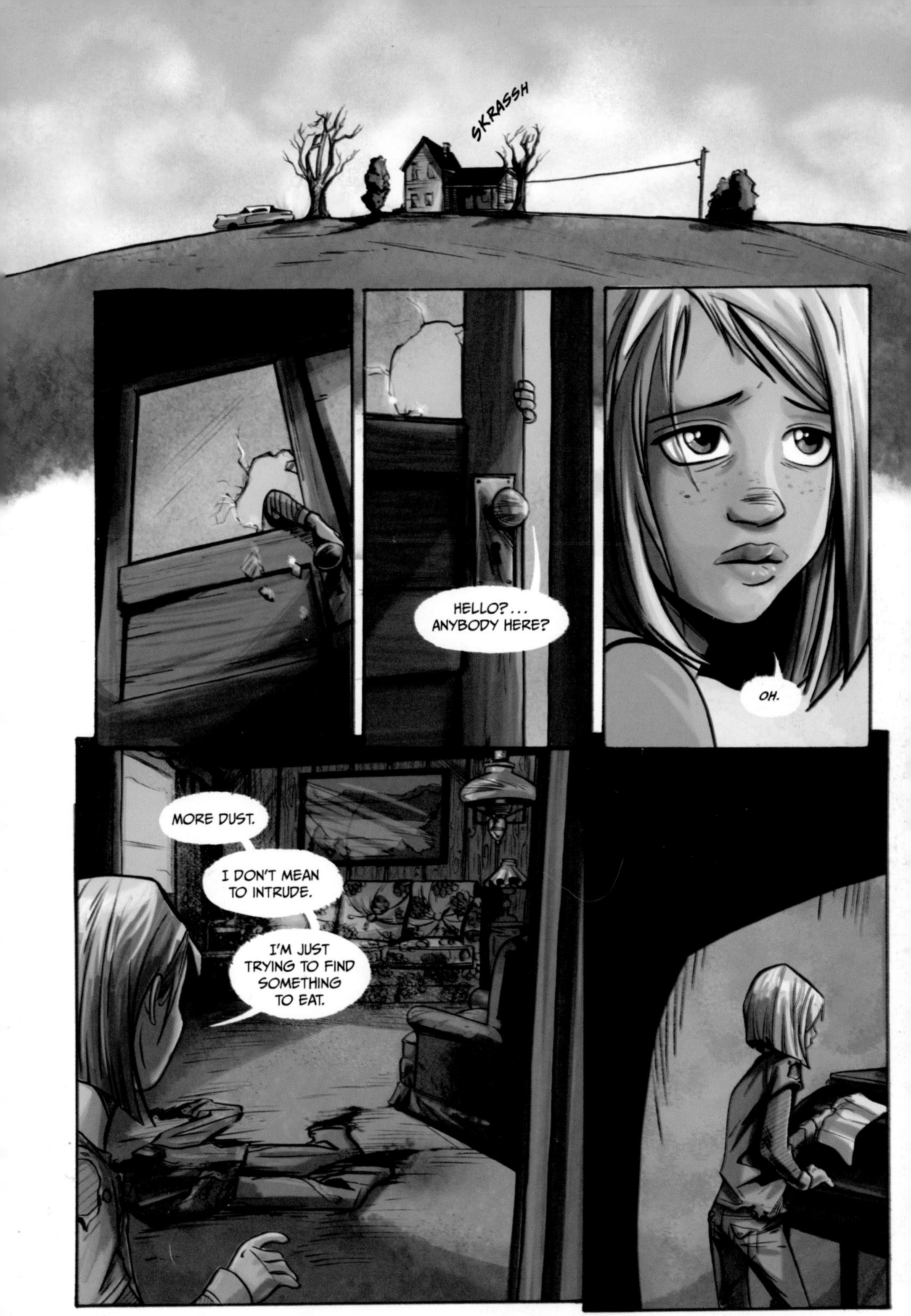

SKRASSH
HELLO?...
ANYBODY HERE?
OH.
MORE DUST.
I DON'T MEAN TO INTRUDE.
I'M JUST TRYING TO FIND SOMETHING TO EAT.

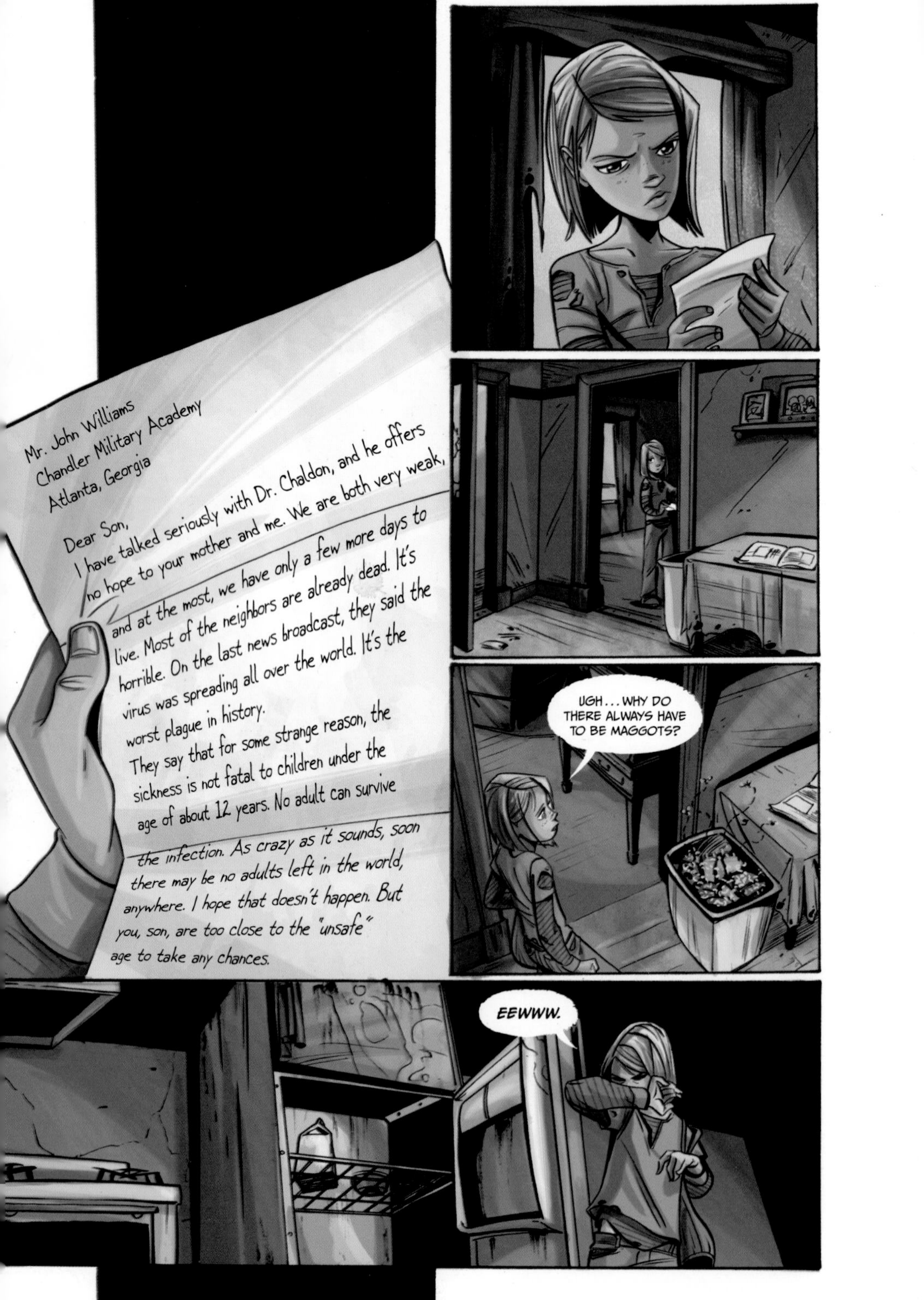
Mr. John Williams
Chandler Military Academy
Atlanta, Georgia
Dear Son,
I have talked seriously with Dr. Chaldon, and he offers no hope to your mother and me. We are both very weak, and at the most, we have only a few more days to live. Most of the neighbors are already dead. It's horrible. On the last news broadcast, they said the virus was spreading all over the world. It's the worst plague in history.
They say that for some strange reason, the sickness is not fatal to children under the age of about 12 years. No adult can survive the infection. As crazy as it sounds, soon there may be no adults left in the world, anywhere. I hope that doesn't happen. But you, son, are too close to the "unsafe" age to take any chances.
UGH... WHY DO THERE ALWAYS HAVE TO BE MAGGOTS?
EEWWW.

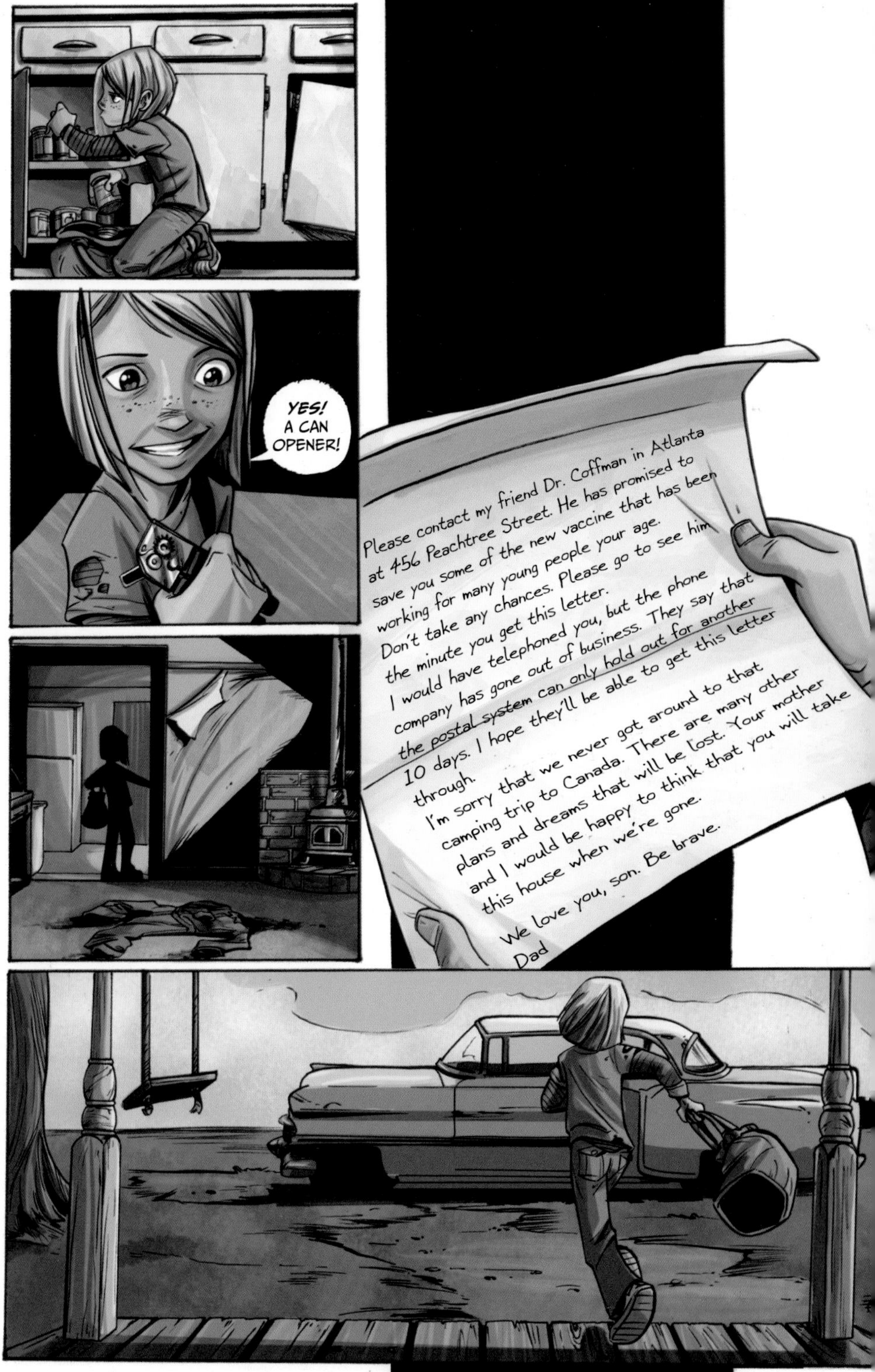
YES! A CAN OPENER!
Please contact my friend Dr. Coffman in Atlanta at 456 Peachtree Street. He has promised to save you some of the new vaccine that has been working for many young people your age. Don't take any chances. Please go to see him the minute you get this letter.
I would have telephoned you, but the phone company has gone out of business. They say that the postal system can only hold out for another 10 days. I hope they'll be able to get this letter through.
I'm sorry that we never got around to that camping trip to Canada. There are many other plans and dreams that will be lost. Your mother and I would be happy to think that you will take this house when we're gone.
We love you, son. Be brave.
Dad

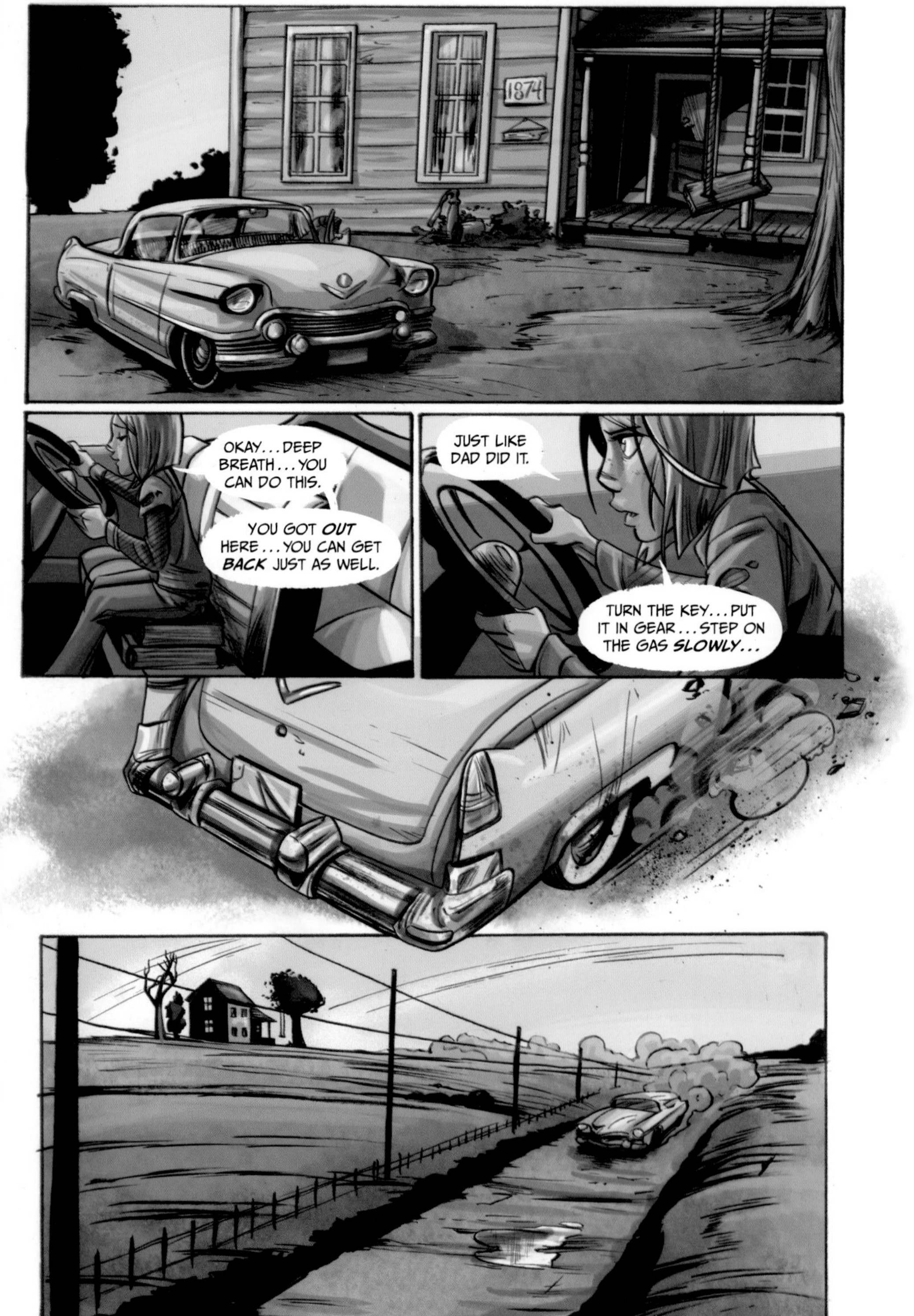
OKAY... DEEP BREATH... YOU CAN DO THIS.
YOU GOT OUT HERE... YOU CAN GET BACK JUST AS WELL.
JUST LIKE DAD DID IT.
TURN THE KEY... PUT IT IN GEAR... STEP ON THE GAS SLOWLY...

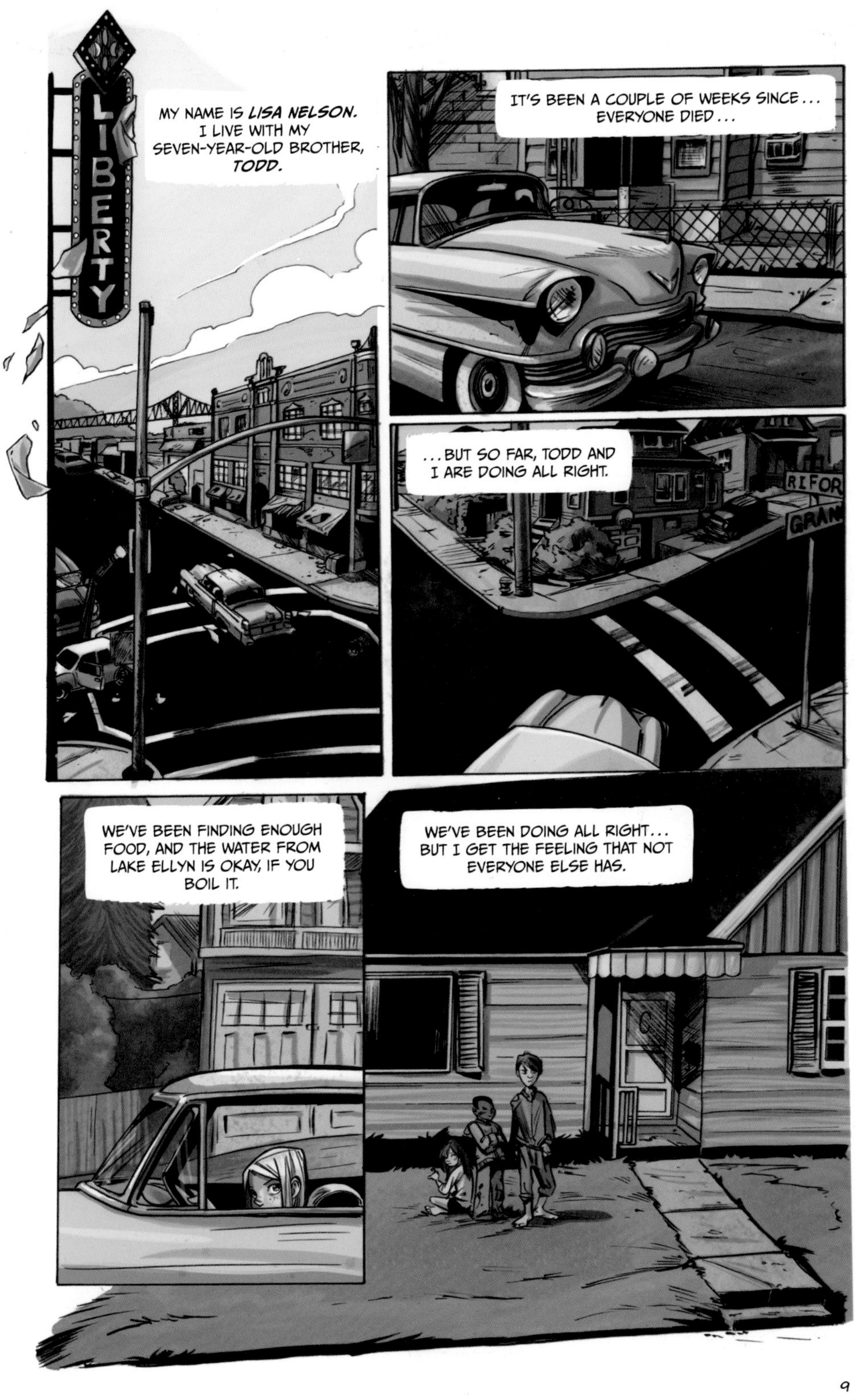
LIBERTY
MY NAME IS *LISA NELSON.* I LIVE WITH MY SEVEN-YEAR-OLD BROTHER, *TODD.*
IT'S BEEN A COUPLE OF WEEKS SINCE... EVERYONE DIED...
...BUT SO FAR, TODD AND I ARE DOING ALL RIGHT.
RIFOR
GRAN
WE'VE BEEN FINDING ENOUGH FOOD, AND THE WATER FROM LAKE ELLYN IS OKAY, IF YOU BOIL IT.
WE'VE BEEN DOING ALL RIGHT... BUT I GET THE FEELING THAT NOT EVERYONE ELSE HAS.

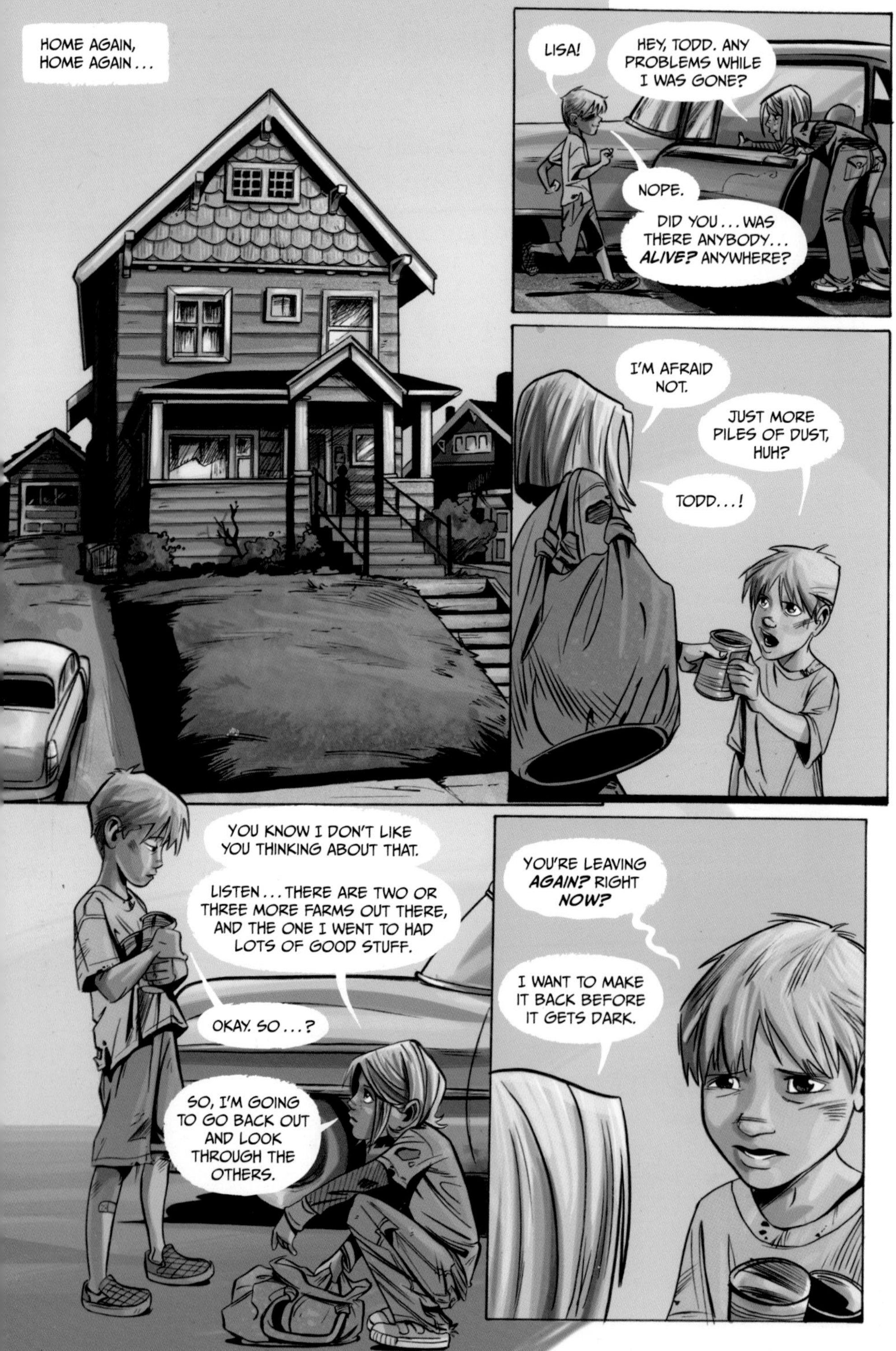
HOME AGAIN, HOME AGAIN...
LISA!
HEY, TODD. ANY PROBLEMS WHILE I WAS GONE?
NOPE.
DID YOU...WAS THERE ANYBODY... *ALIVE?* ANYWHERE?
I'M AFRAID NOT.
JUST MORE PILES OF DUST, HUH?
TODD...!
YOU KNOW I DON'T LIKE YOU THINKING ABOUT THAT.
LISTEN...THERE ARE TWO OR THREE MORE FARMS OUT THERE, AND THE ONE I WENT TO HAD LOTS OF GOOD STUFF.
OKAY. SO...?
SO, I'M GOING TO GO BACK OUT AND LOOK THROUGH THE OTHERS.
YOU'RE LEAVING *AGAIN?* RIGHT *NOW?*
I WANT TO MAKE IT BACK BEFORE IT GETS DARK.

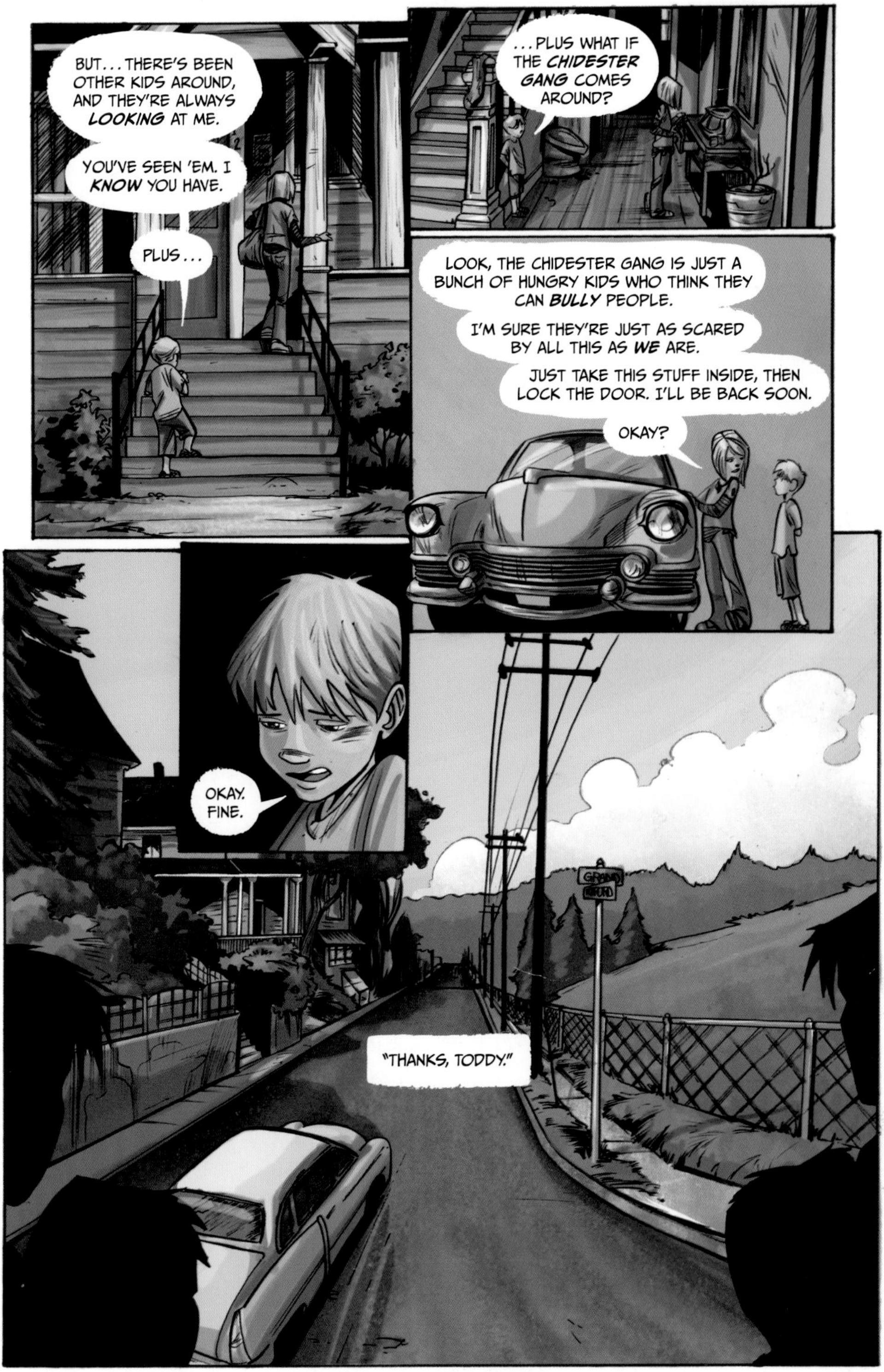
BUT... THERE'S BEEN OTHER KIDS AROUND, AND THEY'RE ALWAYS LOOKING AT ME.
YOU'VE SEEN 'EM. I KNOW YOU HAVE.
PLUS...
...PLUS WHAT IF THE CHIDESTER GANG COMES AROUND?
LOOK, THE CHIDESTER GANG IS JUST A BUNCH OF HUNGRY KIDS WHO THINK THEY CAN BULLY PEOPLE.
I'M SURE THEY'RE JUST AS SCARED BY ALL THIS AS WE ARE.
JUST TAKE THIS STUFF INSIDE, THEN LOCK THE DOOR. I'LL BE BACK SOON.
OKAY?
OKAY. FINE.
"THANKS, TODDY."

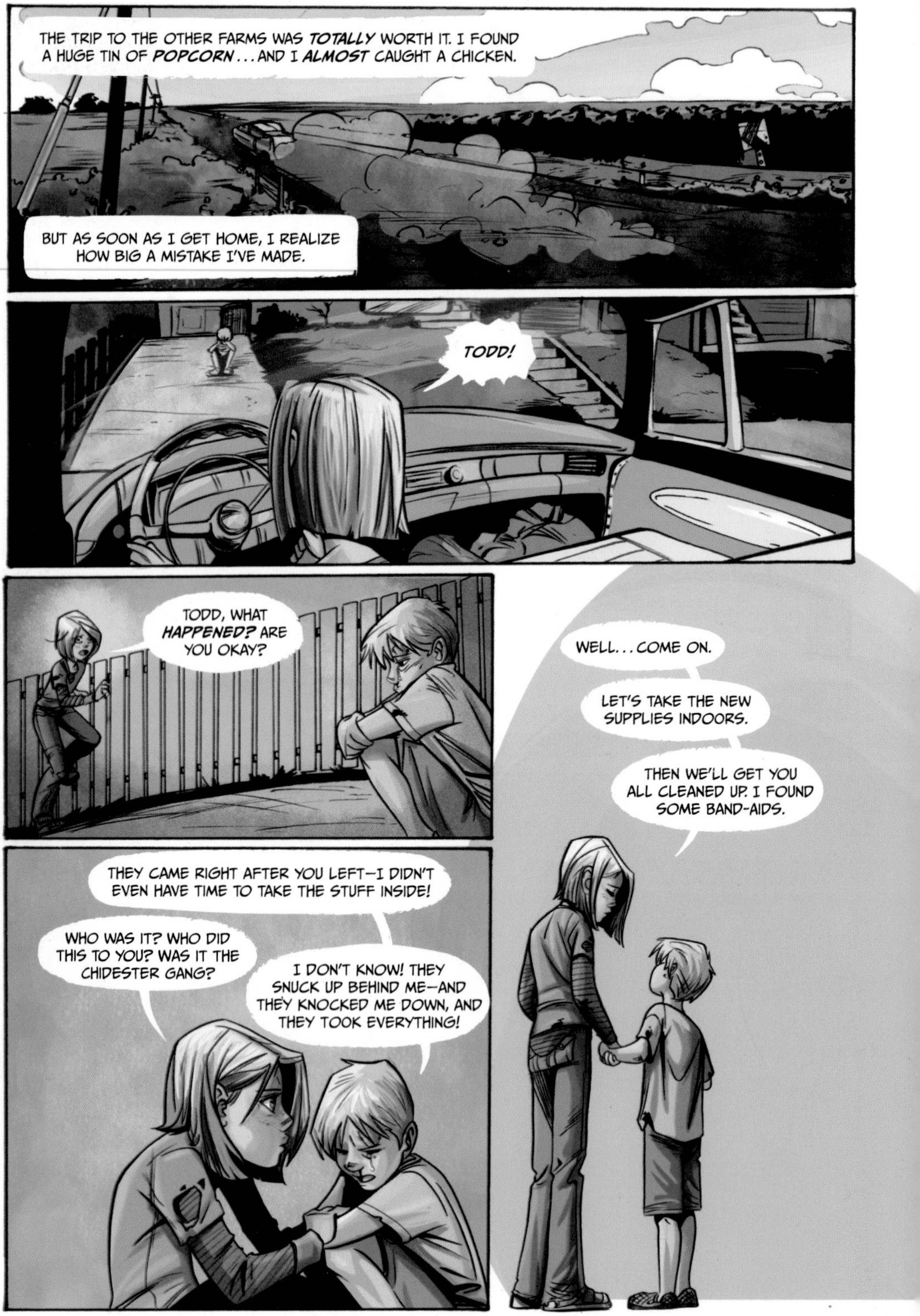
THE TRIP TO THE OTHER FARMS WAS TOTALLY WORTH IT. I FOUND A HUGE TIN OF POPCORN . . . AND I ALMOST CAUGHT A CHICKEN.
BUT AS SOON AS I GET HOME, I REALIZE HOW BIG A MISTAKE I'VE MADE.
TODD!
TODD, WHAT HAPPENED? ARE YOU OKAY?
THEY CAME RIGHT AFTER YOU LEFT—I DIDN'T EVEN HAVE TIME TO TAKE THE STUFF INSIDE!
WHO WAS IT? WHO DID THIS TO YOU? WAS IT THE CHIDESTER GANG?
I DON'T KNOW! THEY SNUCK UP BEHIND ME—AND THEY KNOCKED ME DOWN, AND THEY TOOK EVERYTHING!
WELL. . . COME ON.
LET'S TAKE THE NEW SUPPLIES INDOORS.
THEN WE'LL GET YOU ALL CLEANED UP. I FOUND SOME BAND-AIDS.

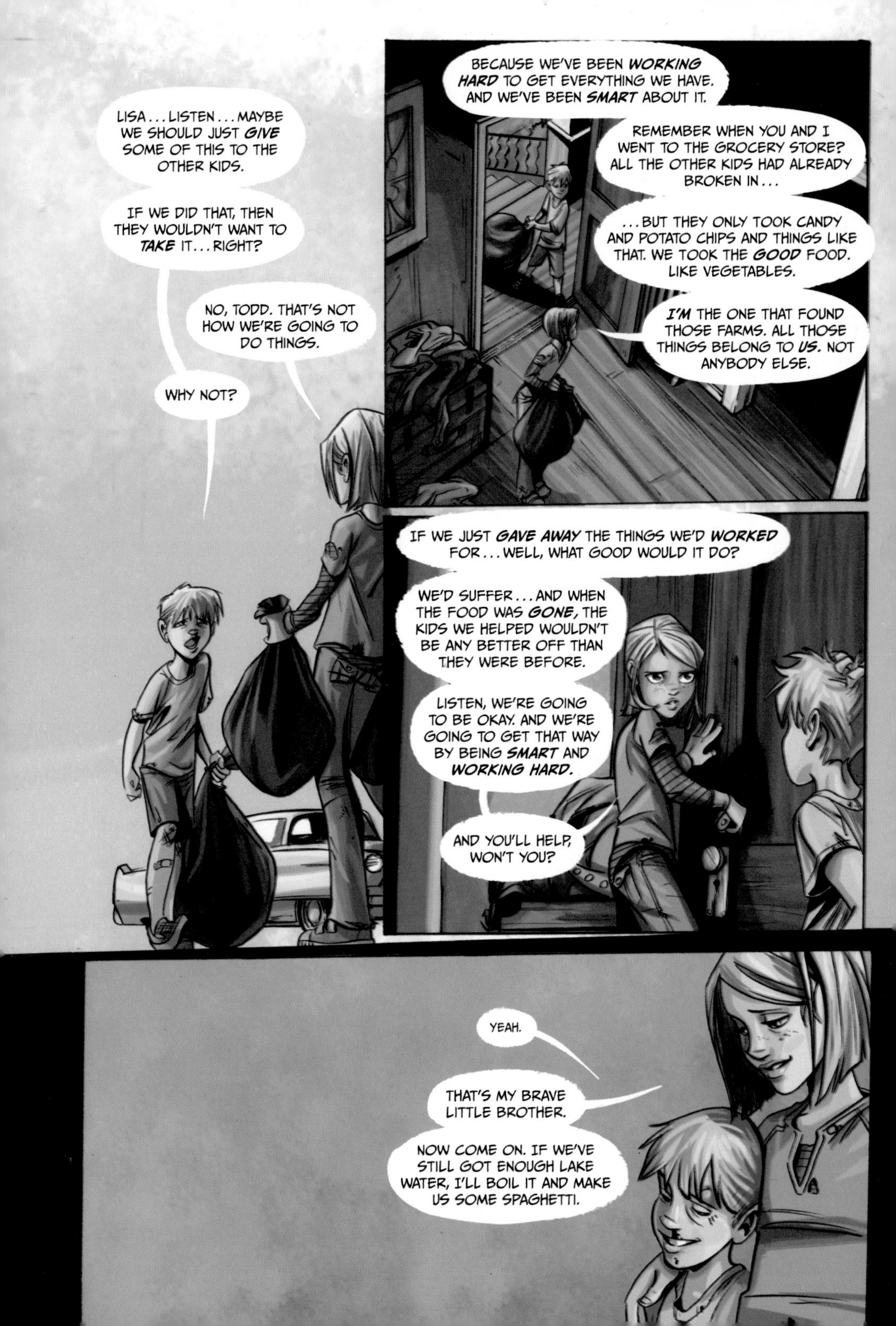

LISA... LISTEN... MAYBE WE SHOULD JUST *GIVE* SOME OF THIS TO THE OTHER KIDS.
IF WE DID THAT, THEN THEY WOULDN'T WANT TO *TAKE* IT... RIGHT?
NO, TODD. THAT'S NOT HOW WE'RE GOING TO DO THINGS.
WHY NOT?
BECAUSE WE'VE BEEN *WORKING HARD* TO GET EVERYTHING WE HAVE. AND WE'VE BEEN *SMART* ABOUT IT.
REMEMBER WHEN YOU AND I WENT TO THE GROCERY STORE? ALL THE OTHER KIDS HAD ALREADY BROKEN IN...
...BUT THEY ONLY TOOK CANDY AND POTATO CHIPS AND THINGS LIKE THAT. WE TOOK THE *GOOD* FOOD. LIKE VEGETABLES.
I'M THE ONE THAT FOUND THOSE FARMS. ALL THOSE THINGS BELONG TO *US.* NOT ANYBODY ELSE.
IF WE JUST *GAVE AWAY* THE THINGS WE'D *WORKED* FOR... WELL, WHAT GOOD WOULD IT DO?
WE'D SUFFER... AND WHEN THE FOOD WAS *GONE,* THE KIDS WE HELPED WOULDN'T BE ANY BETTER OFF THAN THEY WERE BEFORE.
LISTEN, WE'RE GOING TO BE OKAY. AND WE'RE GOING TO GET THAT WAY BY BEING *SMART* AND *WORKING HARD.*
AND YOU'LL HELP, WON'T YOU?
YEAH.
THAT'S MY BRAVE LITTLE BROTHER.
NOW COME ON. IF WE'VE STILL GOT ENOUGH LAKE WATER, I'LL BOIL IT AND MAKE US SOME SPAGHETTI.

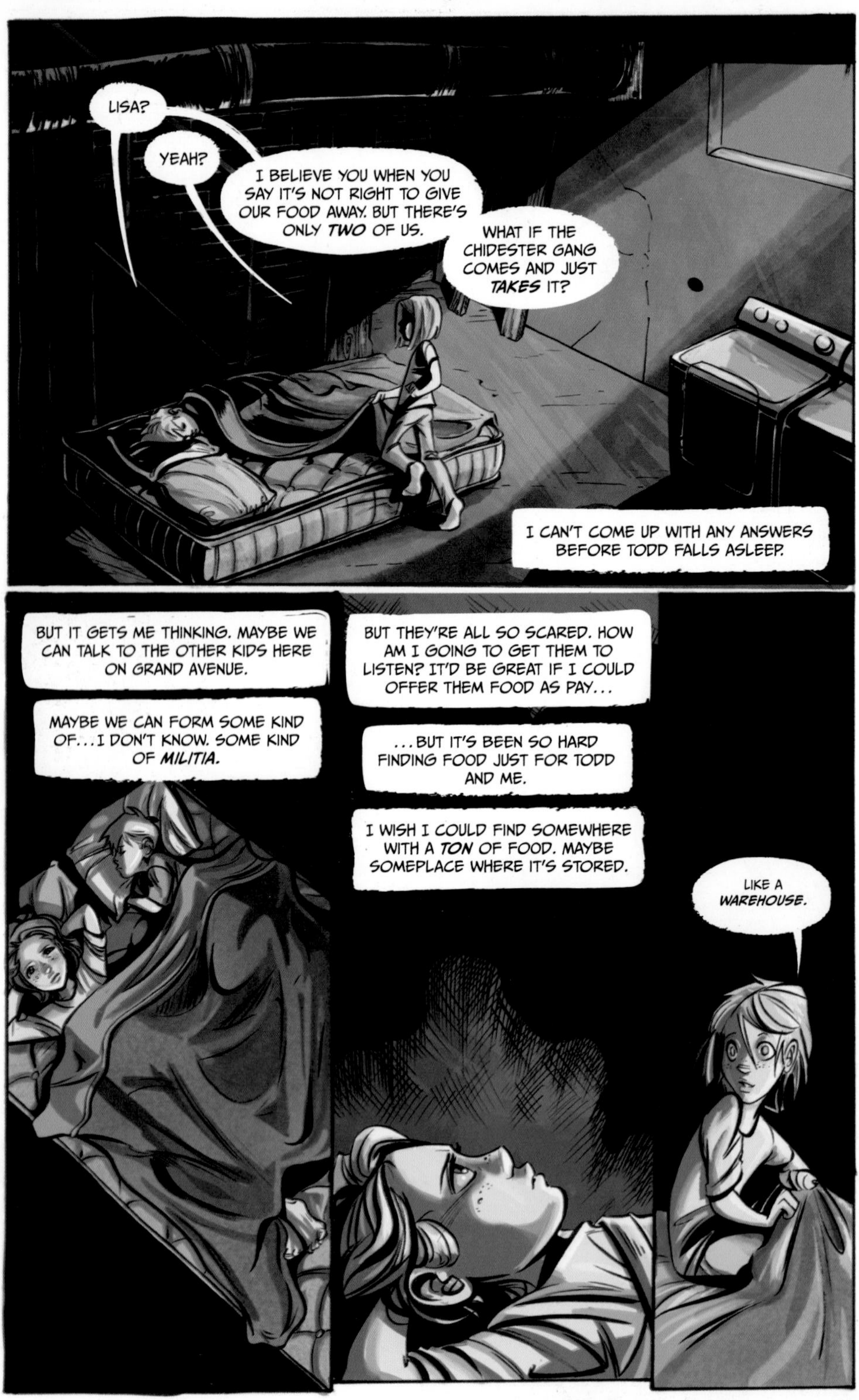
LISA?
YEAH?
I BELIEVE YOU WHEN YOU SAY IT'S NOT RIGHT TO GIVE OUR FOOD AWAY. BUT THERE'S ONLY TWO OF US.
WHAT IF THE CHIDESTER GANG COMES AND JUST TAKES IT?
I CAN'T COME UP WITH ANY ANSWERS BEFORE TODD FALLS ASLEEP.
BUT IT GETS ME THINKING. MAYBE WE CAN TALK TO THE OTHER KIDS HERE ON GRAND AVENUE.
MAYBE WE CAN FORM SOME KIND OF... I DON'T KNOW. SOME KIND OF MILITIA.
BUT THEY'RE ALL SO SCARED. HOW AM I GOING TO GET THEM TO LISTEN? IT'D BE GREAT IF I COULD OFFER THEM FOOD AS PAY...
...BUT IT'S BEEN SO HARD FINDING FOOD JUST FOR TODD AND ME.
I WISH I COULD FIND SOMEWHERE WITH A TON OF FOOD. MAYBE SOMEPLACE WHERE IT'S STORED.
LIKE A WAREHOUSE.

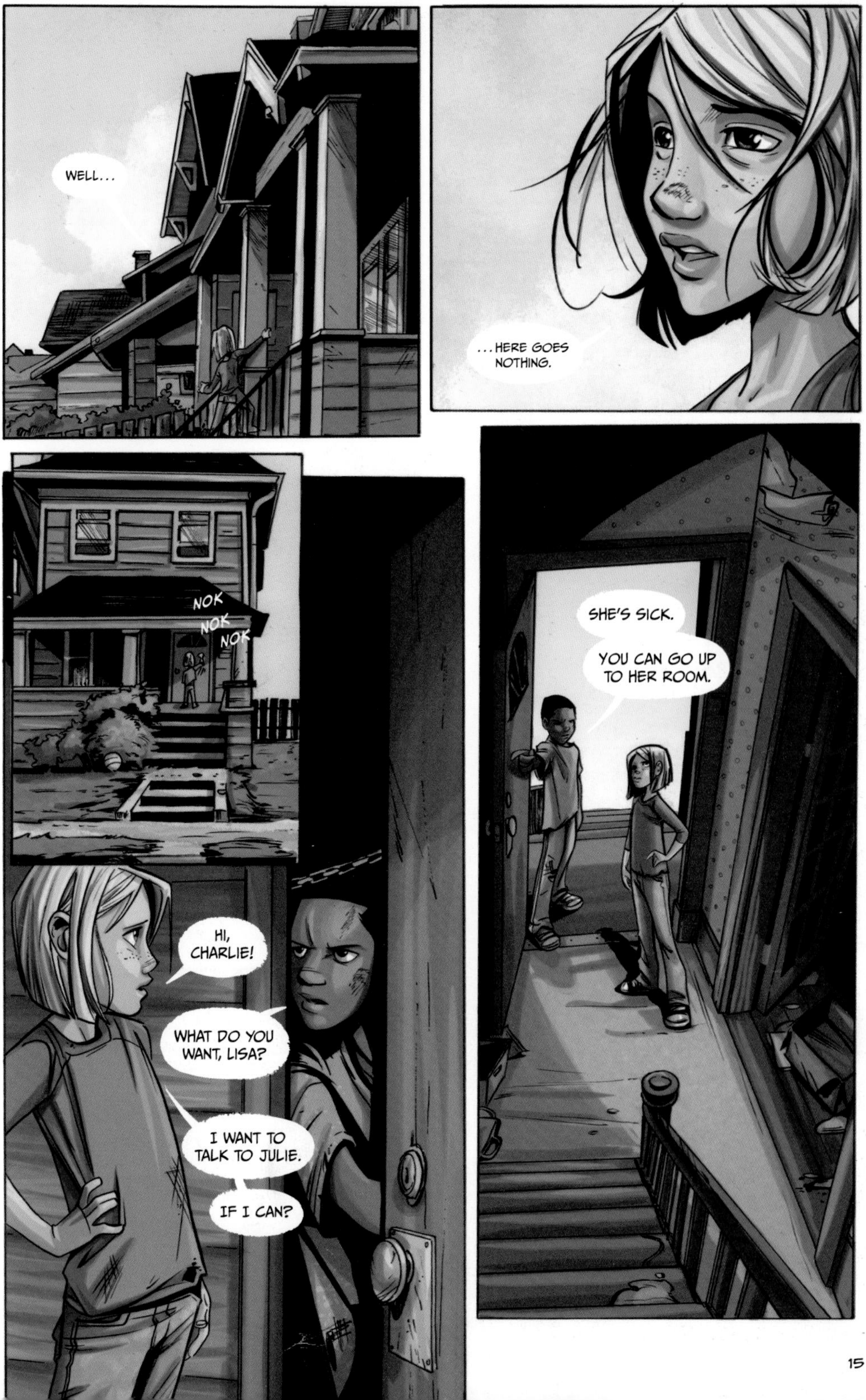
WELL...
...HERE GOES NOTHING.
NOK
NOK
NOK
HI, CHARLIE!
WHAT DO YOU WANT, LISA?
I WANT TO TALK TO JULIE.
IF I CAN?
SHE'S SICK.
YOU CAN GO UP TO HER ROOM.

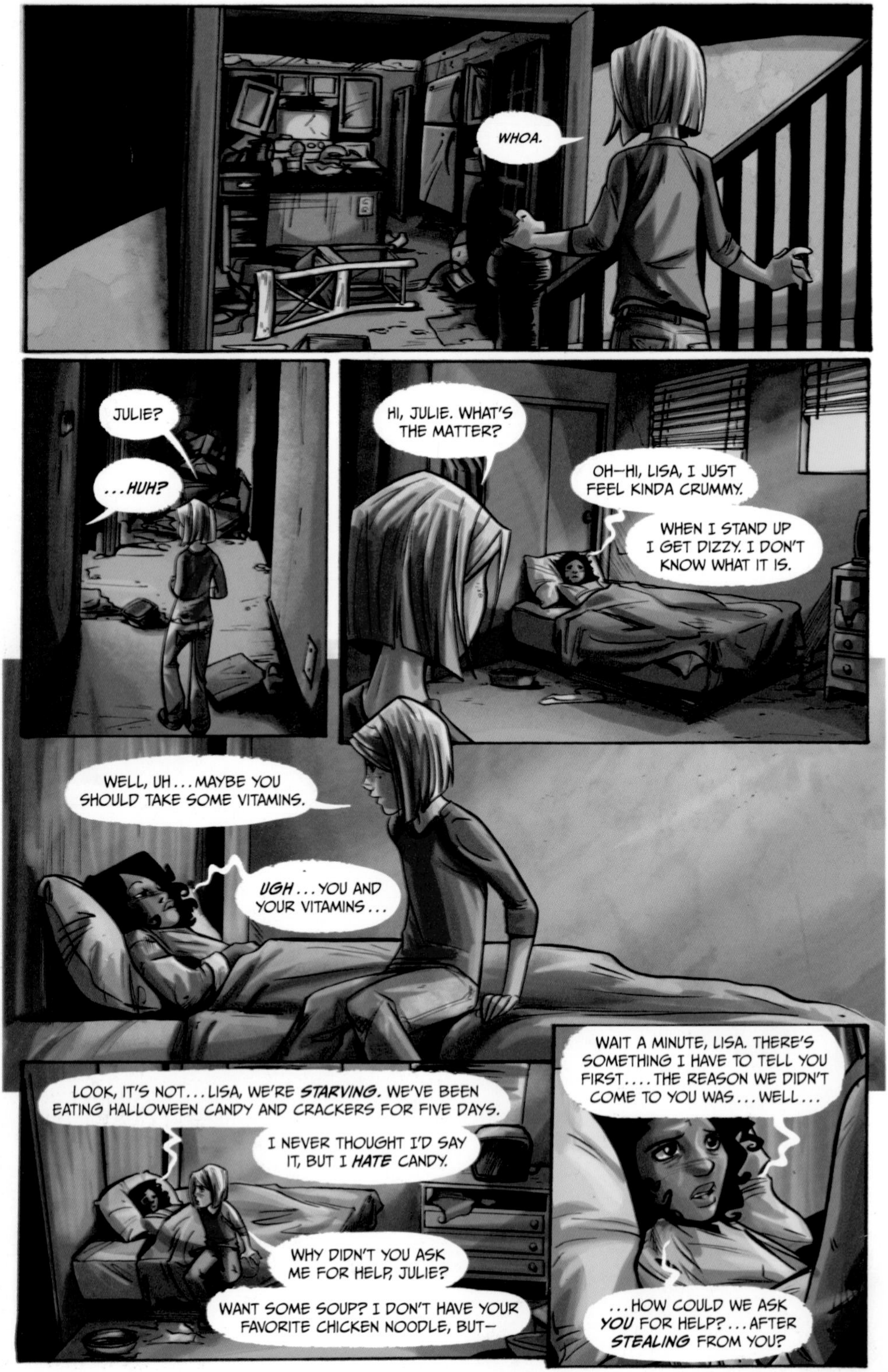
WHOA.
JULIE?
...HUH?
HI, JULIE. WHAT'S THE MATTER?
OH—HI, LISA. I JUST FEEL KINDA CRUMMY.
WHEN I STAND UP I GET DIZZY. I DON'T KNOW WHAT IT IS.
WELL, UH...MAYBE YOU SHOULD TAKE SOME VITAMINS.
UGH...YOU AND YOUR VITAMINS...
LOOK, IT'S NOT...LISA, WE'RE STARVING. WE'VE BEEN EATING HALLOWEEN CANDY AND CRACKERS FOR FIVE DAYS.
I NEVER THOUGHT I'D SAY IT, BUT I HATE CANDY.
WHY DIDN'T YOU ASK ME FOR HELP, JULIE?
WANT SOME SOUP? I DON'T HAVE YOUR FAVORITE CHICKEN NOODLE, BUT—
WAIT A MINUTE, LISA. THERE'S SOMETHING I HAVE TO TELL YOU FIRST....THE REASON WE DIDN'T COME TO YOU WAS...WELL...
...HOW COULD WE ASK YOU FOR HELP?...AFTER STEALING FROM YOU?

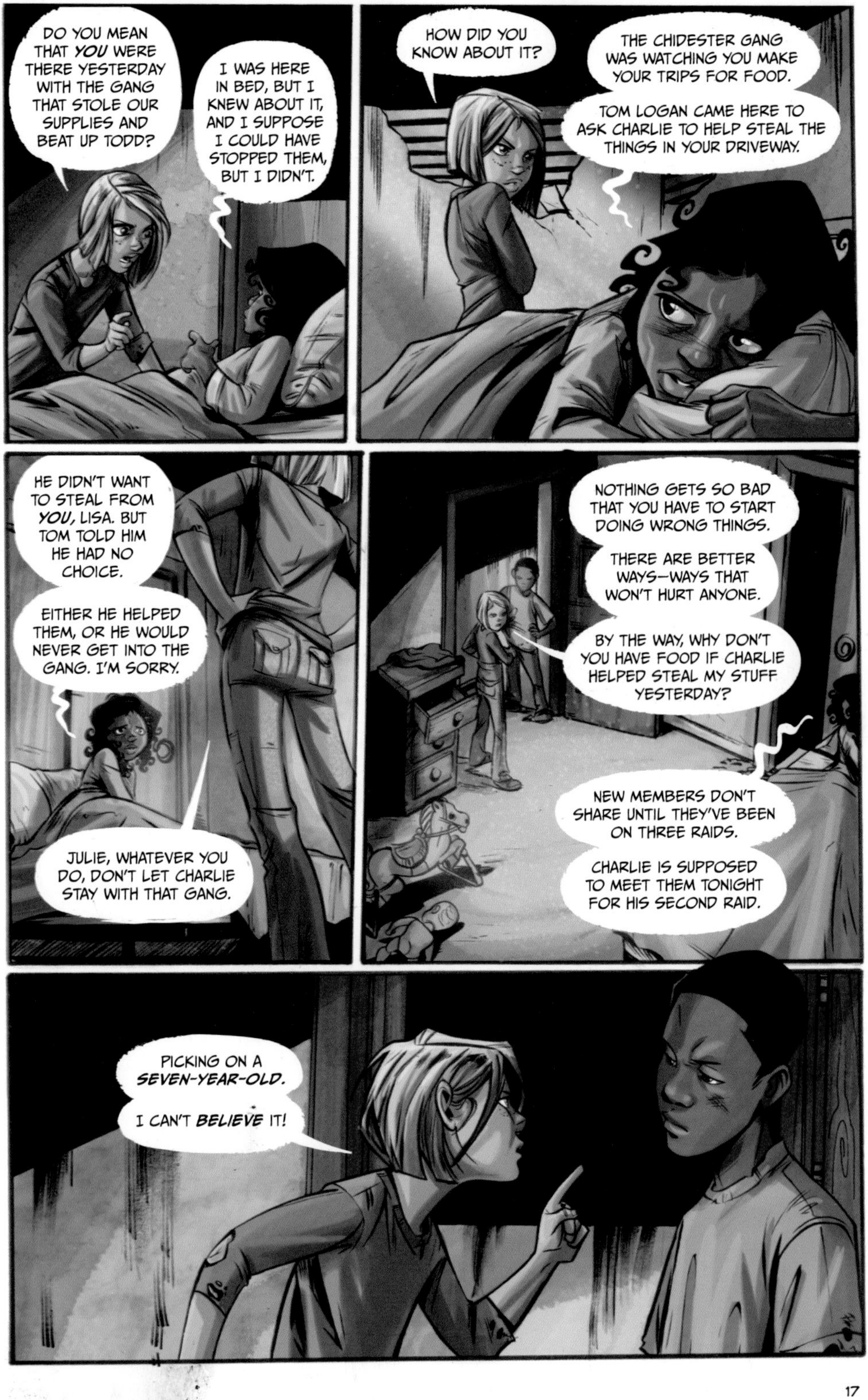
DO YOU MEAN THAT *YOU* WERE THERE YESTERDAY WITH THE GANG THAT STOLE OUR SUPPLIES AND BEAT UP TODD?
I WAS HERE IN BED, BUT I KNEW ABOUT IT, AND I SUPPOSE I COULD HAVE STOPPED THEM, BUT I DIDN'T.
HOW DID YOU KNOW ABOUT IT?
THE CHIDESTER GANG WAS WATCHING YOU MAKE YOUR TRIPS FOR FOOD.
TOM LOGAN CAME HERE TO ASK CHARLIE TO HELP STEAL THE THINGS IN YOUR DRIVEWAY.
HE DIDN'T WANT TO STEAL FROM *YOU*, LISA. BUT TOM TOLD HIM HE HAD NO CHOICE.
EITHER HE HELPED THEM, OR HE WOULD NEVER GET INTO THE GANG. I'M SORRY.
JULIE, WHATEVER YOU DO, DON'T LET CHARLIE STAY WITH THAT GANG.
NOTHING GETS SO BAD THAT YOU HAVE TO START DOING WRONG THINGS.
THERE ARE BETTER WAYS—WAYS THAT WON'T HURT ANYONE.
BY THE WAY, WHY DON'T YOU HAVE FOOD IF CHARLIE HELPED STEAL MY STUFF YESTERDAY?
NEW MEMBERS DON'T SHARE UNTIL THEY'VE BEEN ON THREE RAIDS.
CHARLIE IS SUPPOSED TO MEET THEM TONIGHT FOR HIS SECOND RAID.
PICKING ON A *SEVEN-YEAR-OLD.*
I CAN'T *BELIEVE* IT!

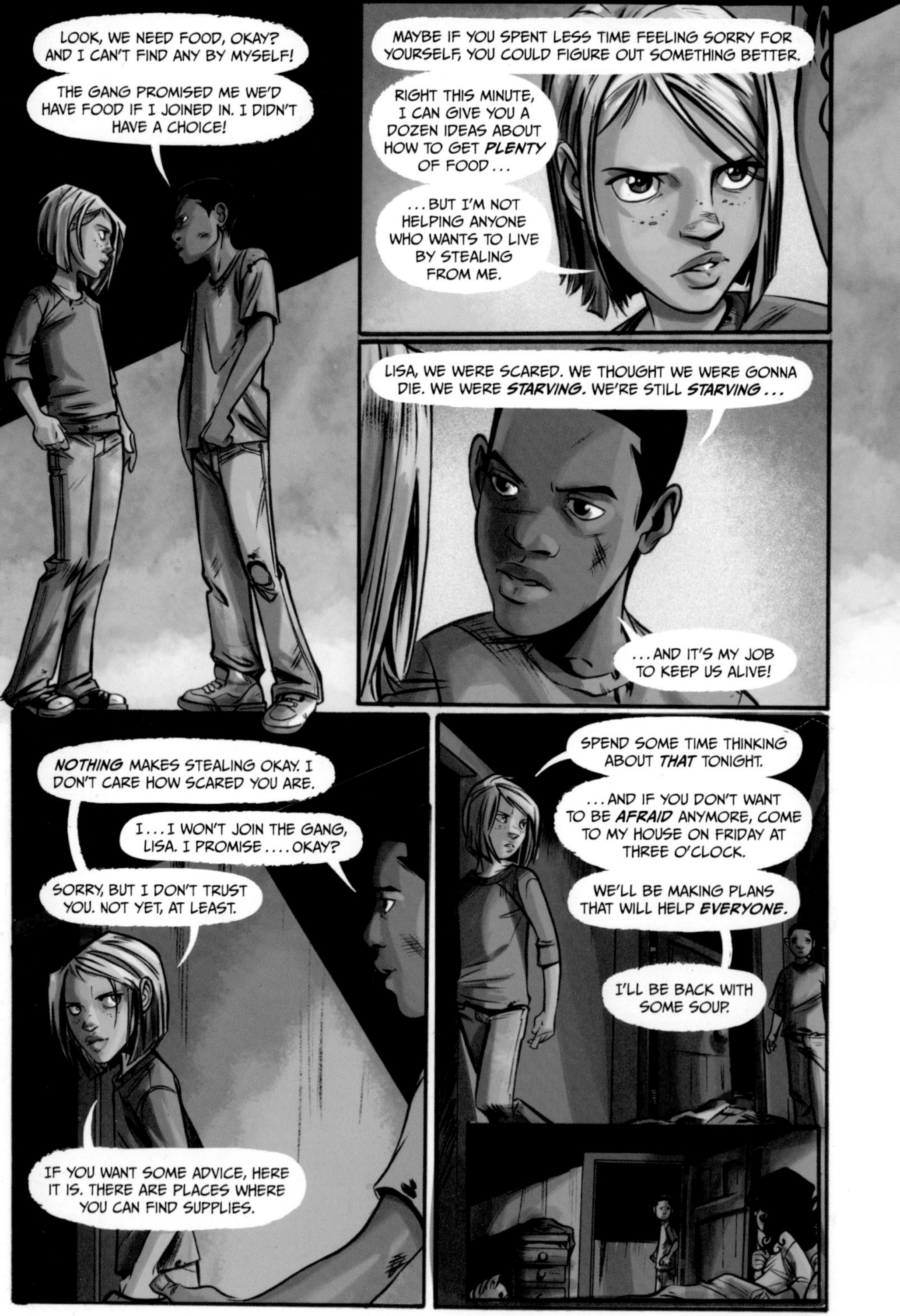

LOOK, WE NEED FOOD, OKAY? AND I CAN'T FIND ANY BY MYSELF!
THE GANG PROMISED ME WE'D HAVE FOOD IF I JOINED IN. I DIDN'T HAVE A CHOICE!
MAYBE IF YOU SPENT LESS TIME FEELING SORRY FOR YOURSELF, YOU COULD FIGURE OUT SOMETHING BETTER.
RIGHT THIS MINUTE, I CAN GIVE YOU A DOZEN IDEAS ABOUT HOW TO GET *PLENTY* OF FOOD . . .
. . . BUT I'M NOT HELPING ANYONE WHO WANTS TO LIVE BY STEALING FROM ME.
LISA, WE WERE SCARED. WE THOUGHT WE WERE GONNA DIE. WE WERE *STARVING.* WE'RE STILL *STARVING . . .*
. . . AND IT'S MY JOB TO KEEP US ALIVE!
NOTHING MAKES STEALING OKAY. I DON'T CARE HOW SCARED YOU ARE.
I . . . I WON'T JOIN THE GANG, LISA. I PROMISE . . . . OKAY?
SORRY, BUT I DON'T TRUST YOU. NOT YET, AT LEAST.
IF YOU WANT SOME ADVICE, HERE IT IS. THERE ARE PLACES WHERE YOU CAN FIND SUPPLIES.
SPEND SOME TIME THINKING ABOUT *THAT* TONIGHT.
. . . AND IF YOU DON'T WANT TO BE *AFRAID* ANYMORE, COME TO MY HOUSE ON FRIDAY AT THREE O'CLOCK.
WE'LL BE MAKING PLANS THAT WILL HELP *EVERYONE.*
I'LL BE BACK WITH SOME SOUP.

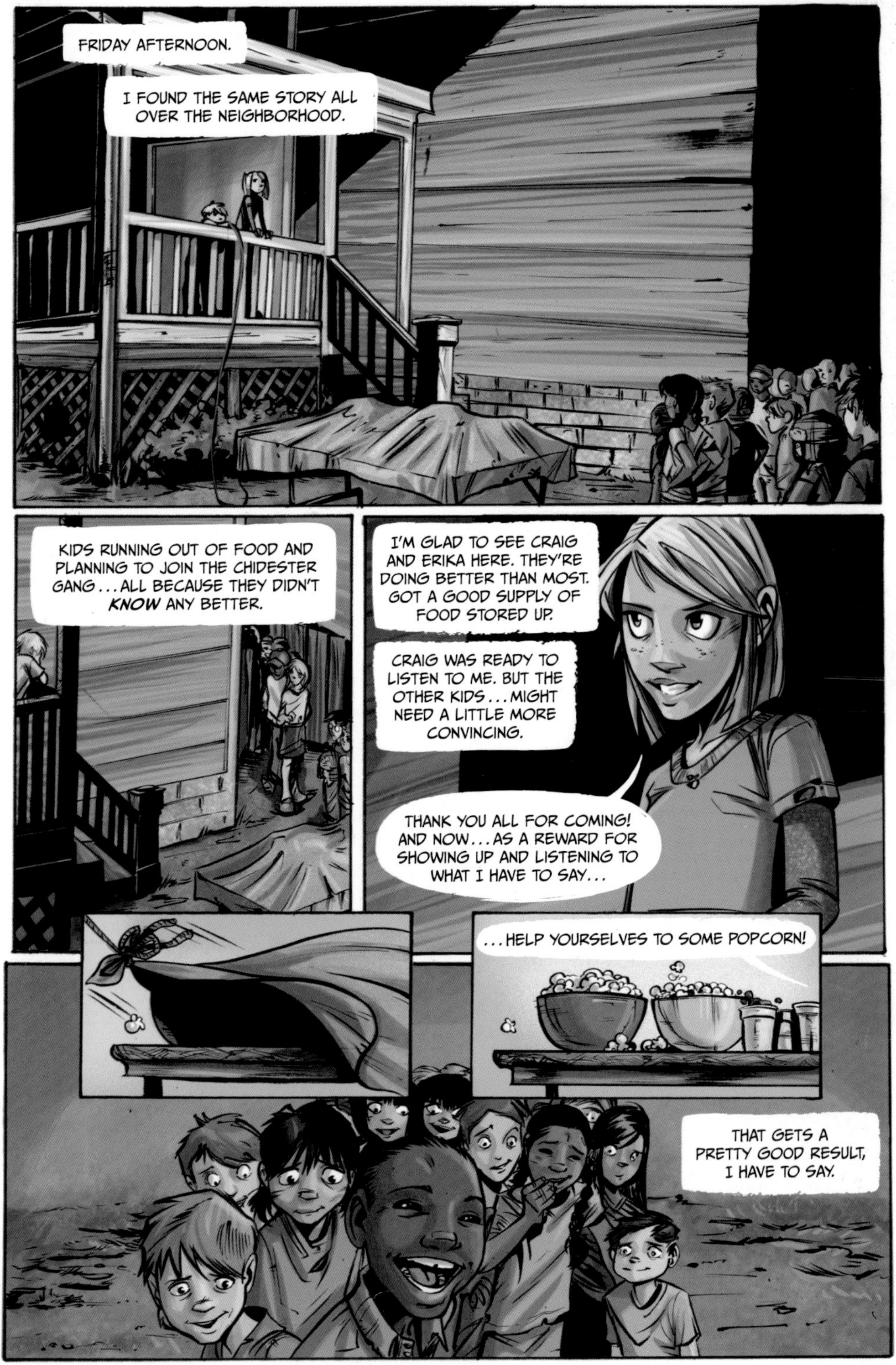
FRIDAY AFTERNOON.
I FOUND THE SAME STORY ALL OVER THE NEIGHBORHOOD.
KIDS RUNNING OUT OF FOOD AND PLANNING TO JOIN THE CHIDESTER GANG... ALL BECAUSE THEY DIDN'T *KNOW* ANY BETTER.
I'M GLAD TO SEE CRAIG AND ERIKA HERE. THEY'RE DOING BETTER THAN MOST. GOT A GOOD SUPPLY OF FOOD STORED UP.
CRAIG WAS READY TO LISTEN TO ME. BUT THE OTHER KIDS... MIGHT NEED A LITTLE MORE CONVINCING.
THANK YOU ALL FOR COMING! AND NOW... AS A REWARD FOR SHOWING UP AND LISTENING TO WHAT I HAVE TO SAY...
...HELP YOURSELVES TO SOME POPCORN!
THAT GETS A PRETTY GOOD RESULT, I HAVE TO SAY.

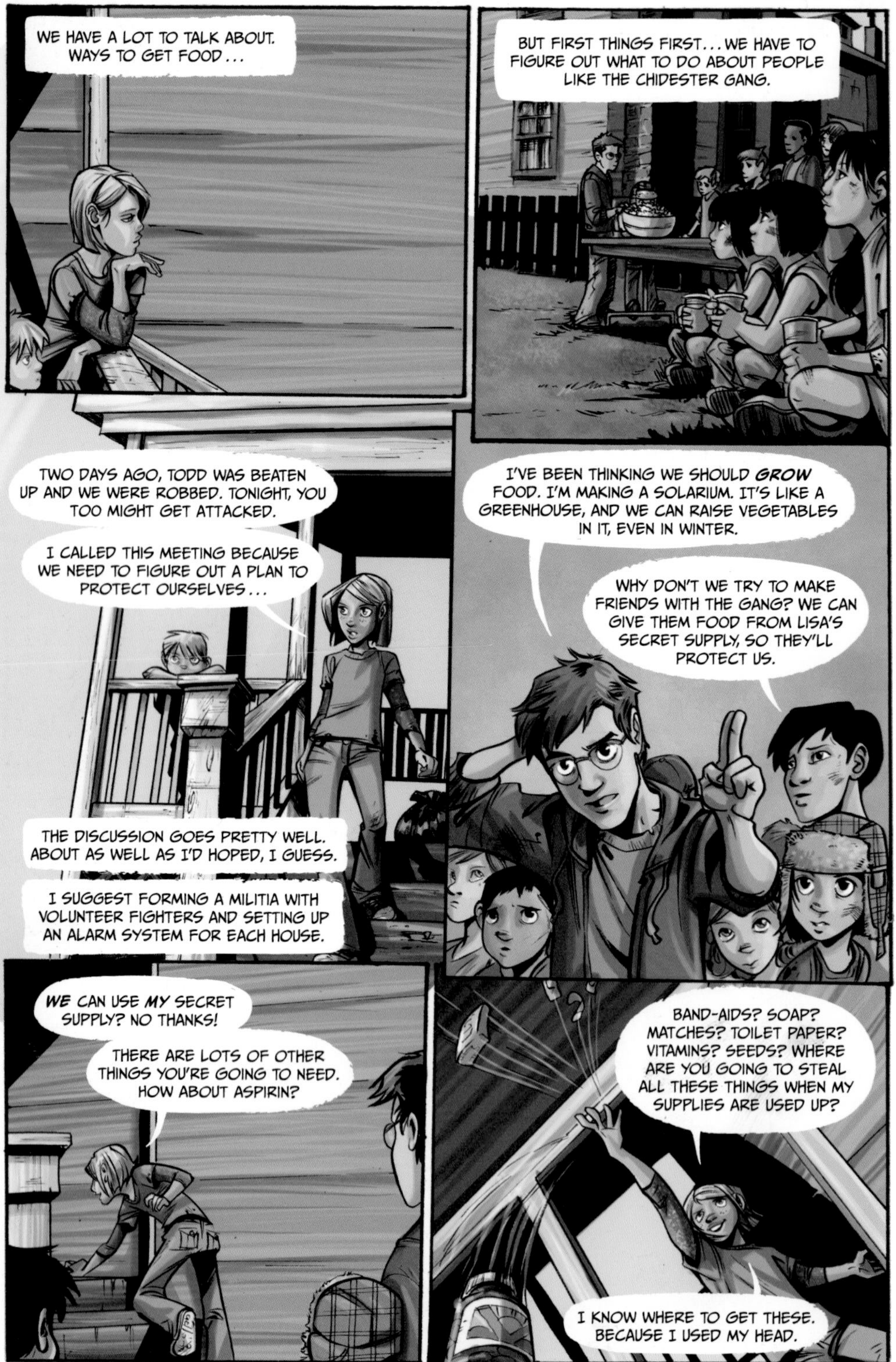
WE HAVE A LOT TO TALK ABOUT. WAYS TO GET FOOD...
BUT FIRST THINGS FIRST...WE HAVE TO FIGURE OUT WHAT TO DO ABOUT PEOPLE LIKE THE CHIDESTER GANG.
TWO DAYS AGO, TODD WAS BEATEN UP AND WE WERE ROBBED. TONIGHT, YOU TOO MIGHT GET ATTACKED.
I CALLED THIS MEETING BECAUSE WE NEED TO FIGURE OUT A PLAN TO PROTECT OURSELVES...
THE DISCUSSION GOES PRETTY WELL. ABOUT AS WELL AS I'D HOPED, I GUESS.
I SUGGEST FORMING A MILITIA WITH VOLUNTEER FIGHTERS AND SETTING UP AN ALARM SYSTEM FOR EACH HOUSE.
I'VE BEEN THINKING WE SHOULD GROW FOOD. I'M MAKING A SOLARIUM. IT'S LIKE A GREENHOUSE, AND WE CAN RAISE VEGETABLES IN IT, EVEN IN WINTER.
WHY DON'T WE TRY TO MAKE FRIENDS WITH THE GANG? WE CAN GIVE THEM FOOD FROM LISA'S SECRET SUPPLY, SO THEY'LL PROTECT US.
WE CAN USE MY SECRET SUPPLY? NO THANKS!
THERE ARE LOTS OF OTHER THINGS YOU'RE GOING TO NEED. HOW ABOUT ASPIRIN?
BAND-AIDS? SOAP? MATCHES? TOILET PAPER? VITAMINS? SEEDS? WHERE ARE YOU GOING TO STEAL ALL THESE THINGS WHEN MY SUPPLIES ARE USED UP?
I KNOW WHERE TO GET THESE. BECAUSE I USED MY HEAD.

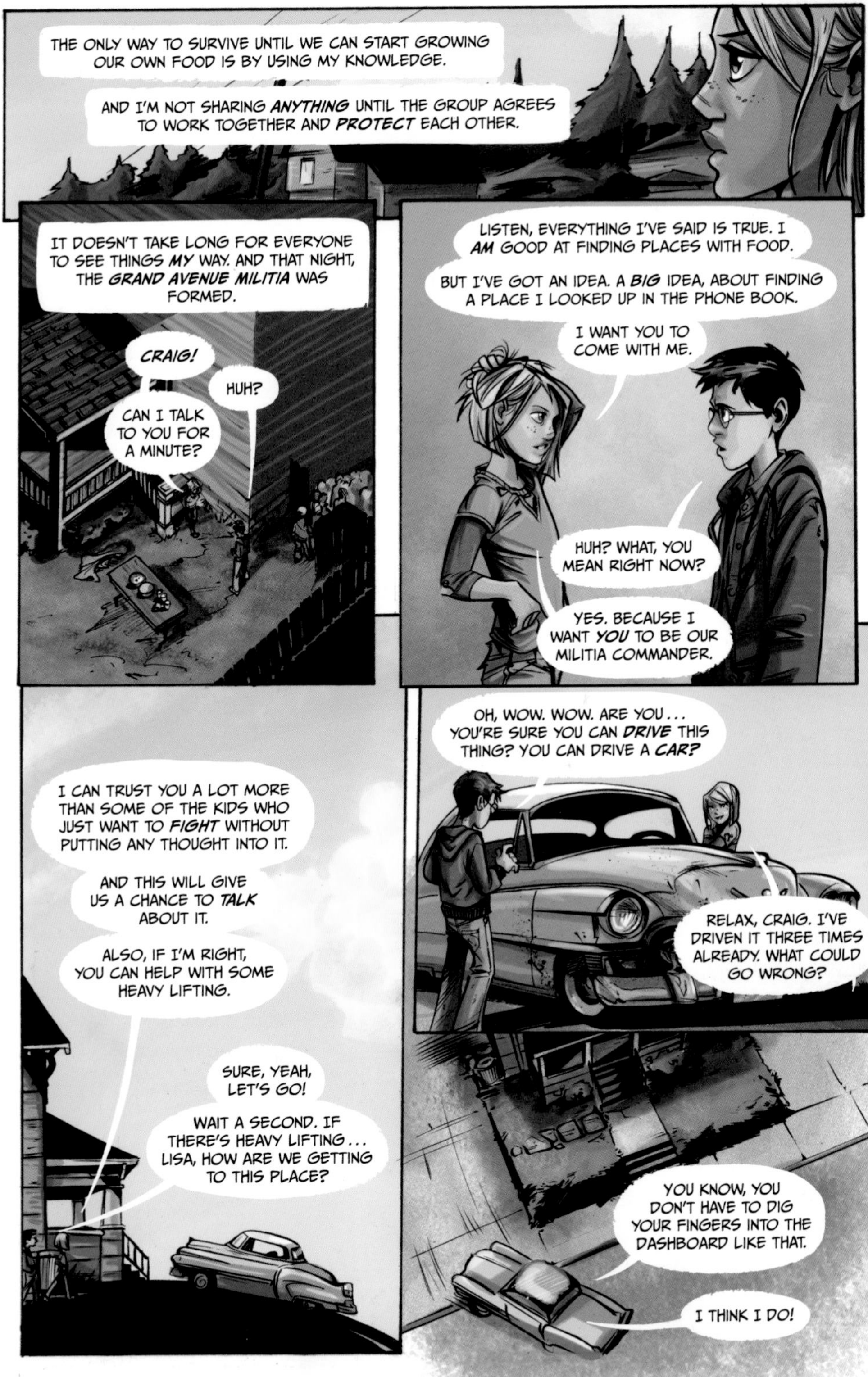
THE ONLY WAY TO SURVIVE UNTIL WE CAN START GROWING OUR OWN FOOD IS BY USING MY KNOWLEDGE.
AND I'M NOT SHARING ANYTHING UNTIL THE GROUP AGREES TO WORK TOGETHER AND PROTECT EACH OTHER.
IT DOESN'T TAKE LONG FOR EVERYONE TO SEE THINGS MY WAY. AND THAT NIGHT, THE GRAND AVENUE MILITIA WAS FORMED.
CRAIG!
HUH?
CAN I TALK TO YOU FOR A MINUTE?
LISTEN, EVERYTHING I'VE SAID IS TRUE. I AM GOOD AT FINDING PLACES WITH FOOD.
BUT I'VE GOT AN IDEA. A BIG IDEA, ABOUT FINDING A PLACE I LOOKED UP IN THE PHONE BOOK.
I WANT YOU TO COME WITH ME.
HUH? WHAT, YOU MEAN RIGHT NOW?
YES. BECAUSE I WANT YOU TO BE OUR MILITIA COMMANDER.
I CAN TRUST YOU A LOT MORE THAN SOME OF THE KIDS WHO JUST WANT TO FIGHT WITHOUT PUTTING ANY THOUGHT INTO IT.
AND THIS WILL GIVE US A CHANCE TO TALK ABOUT IT.
ALSO, IF I'M RIGHT, YOU CAN HELP WITH SOME HEAVY LIFTING.
SURE, YEAH, LET'S GO!
WAIT A SECOND. IF THERE'S HEAVY LIFTING . . . LISA, HOW ARE WE GETTING TO THIS PLACE?
OH, WOW. WOW. ARE YOU . . . YOU'RE SURE YOU CAN DRIVE THIS THING? YOU CAN DRIVE A CAR?
RELAX, CRAIG. I'VE DRIVEN IT THREE TIMES ALREADY. WHAT COULD GO WRONG?
YOU KNOW, YOU DON'T HAVE TO DIG YOUR FINGERS INTO THE DASHBOARD LIKE THAT.
I THINK I DO!

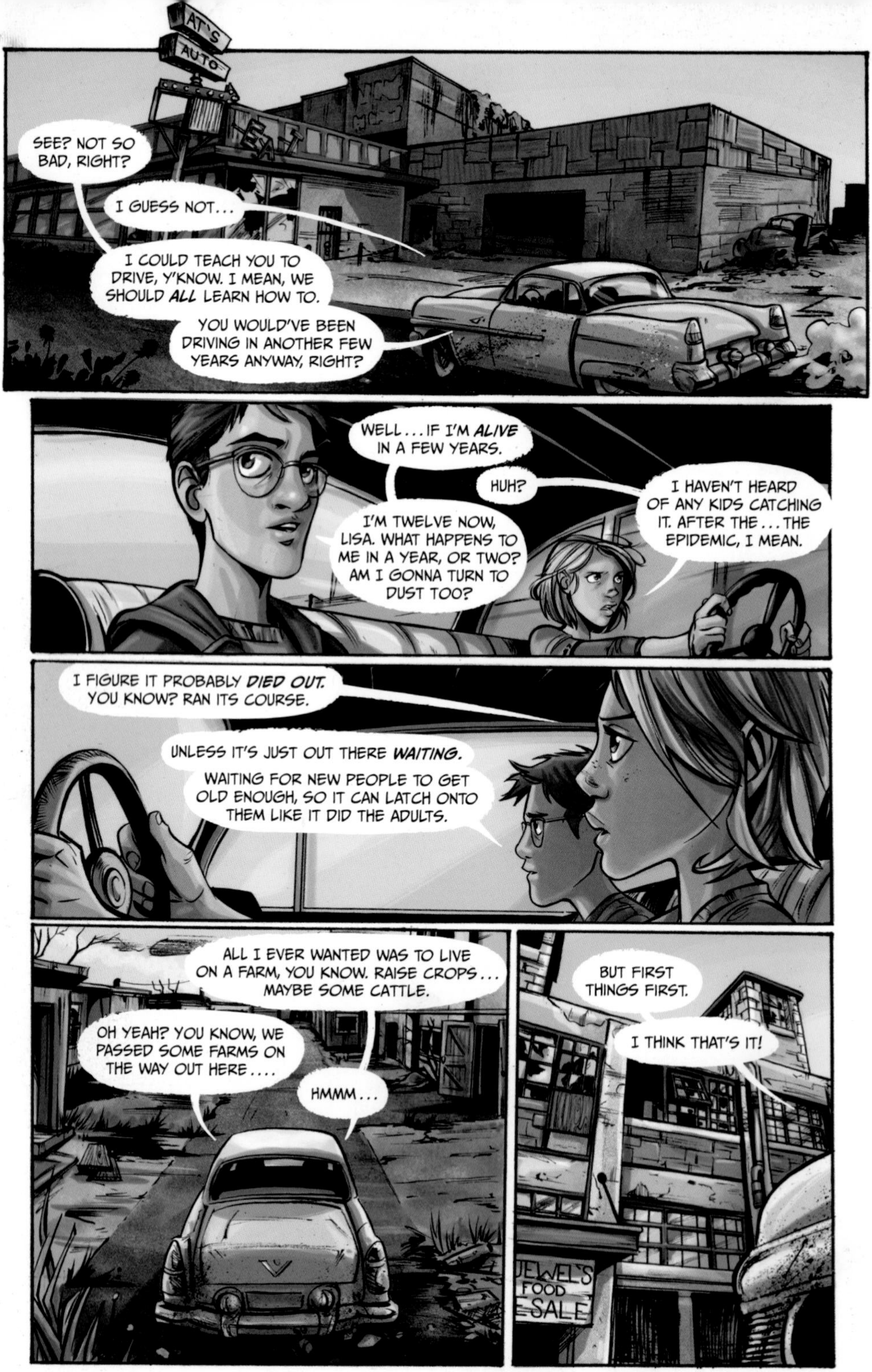
AT'S
AUTO
EAT
SEE? NOT SO BAD, RIGHT?
I GUESS NOT...
I COULD TEACH YOU TO DRIVE, Y'KNOW. I MEAN, WE SHOULD ALL LEARN HOW TO.
YOU WOULD'VE BEEN DRIVING IN ANOTHER FEW YEARS ANYWAY, RIGHT?
WELL... IF I'M ALIVE IN A FEW YEARS.
HUH?
I'M TWELVE NOW, LISA. WHAT HAPPENS TO ME IN A YEAR, OR TWO? AM I GONNA TURN TO DUST TOO?
I HAVEN'T HEARD OF ANY KIDS CATCHING IT. AFTER THE... THE EPIDEMIC, I MEAN.
I FIGURE IT PROBABLY DIED OUT. YOU KNOW? RAN ITS COURSE.
UNLESS IT'S JUST OUT THERE WAITING.
WAITING FOR NEW PEOPLE TO GET OLD ENOUGH, SO IT CAN LATCH ONTO THEM LIKE IT DID THE ADULTS.
ALL I EVER WANTED WAS TO LIVE ON A FARM, YOU KNOW. RAISE CROPS... MAYBE SOME CATTLE.
OH YEAH? YOU KNOW, WE PASSED SOME FARMS ON THE WAY OUT HERE....
HMMM...
BUT FIRST THINGS FIRST.
I THINK THAT'S IT!
JEWEL'S FOOD
SALE

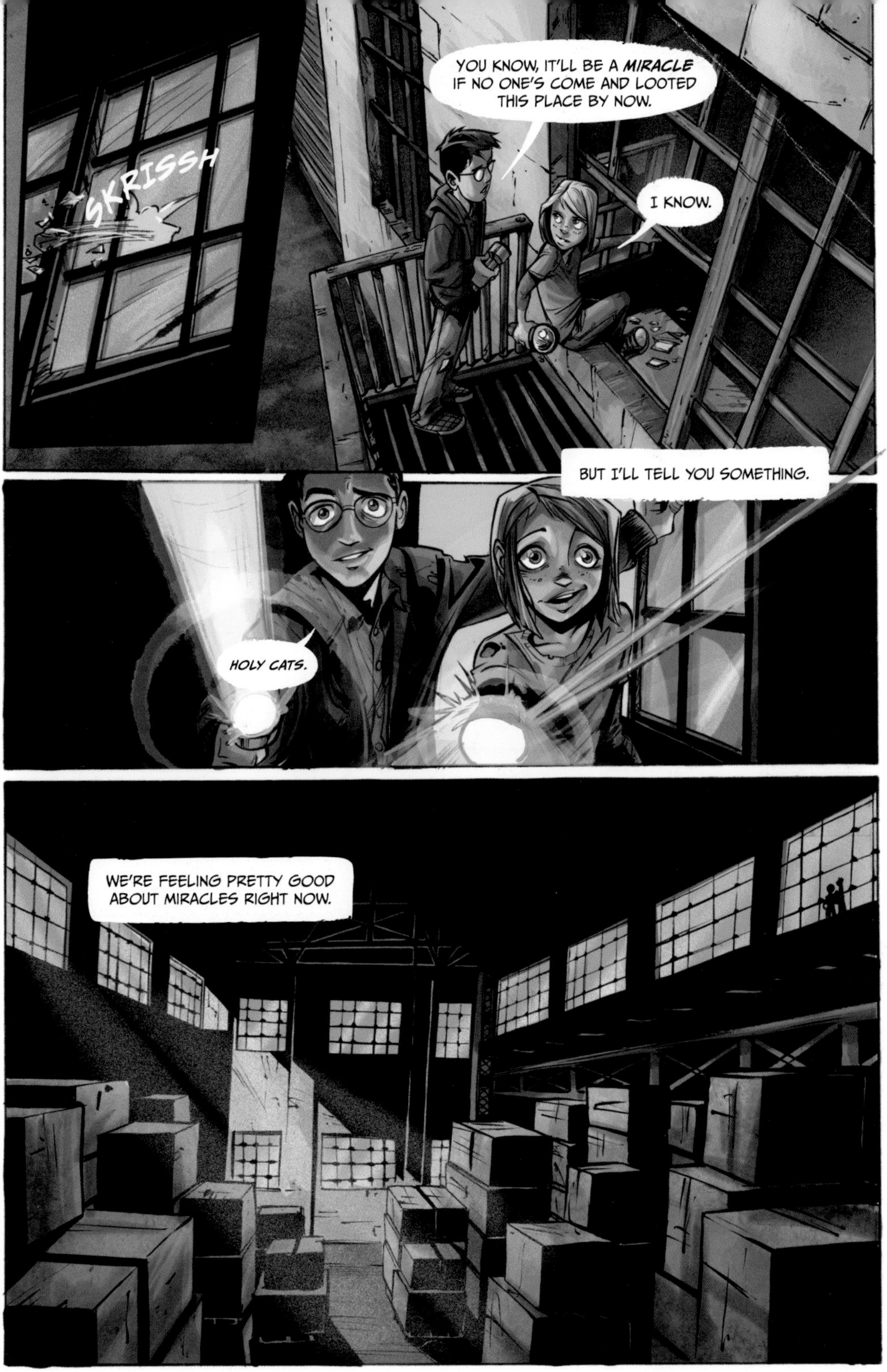
YOU KNOW, IT'LL BE A MIRACLE IF NO ONE'S COME AND LOOTED THIS PLACE BY NOW.
SKRISSH
I KNOW.
BUT I'LL TELL YOU SOMETHING.
HOLY CATS.
WE'RE FEELING PRETTY GOOD ABOUT MIRACLES RIGHT NOW.

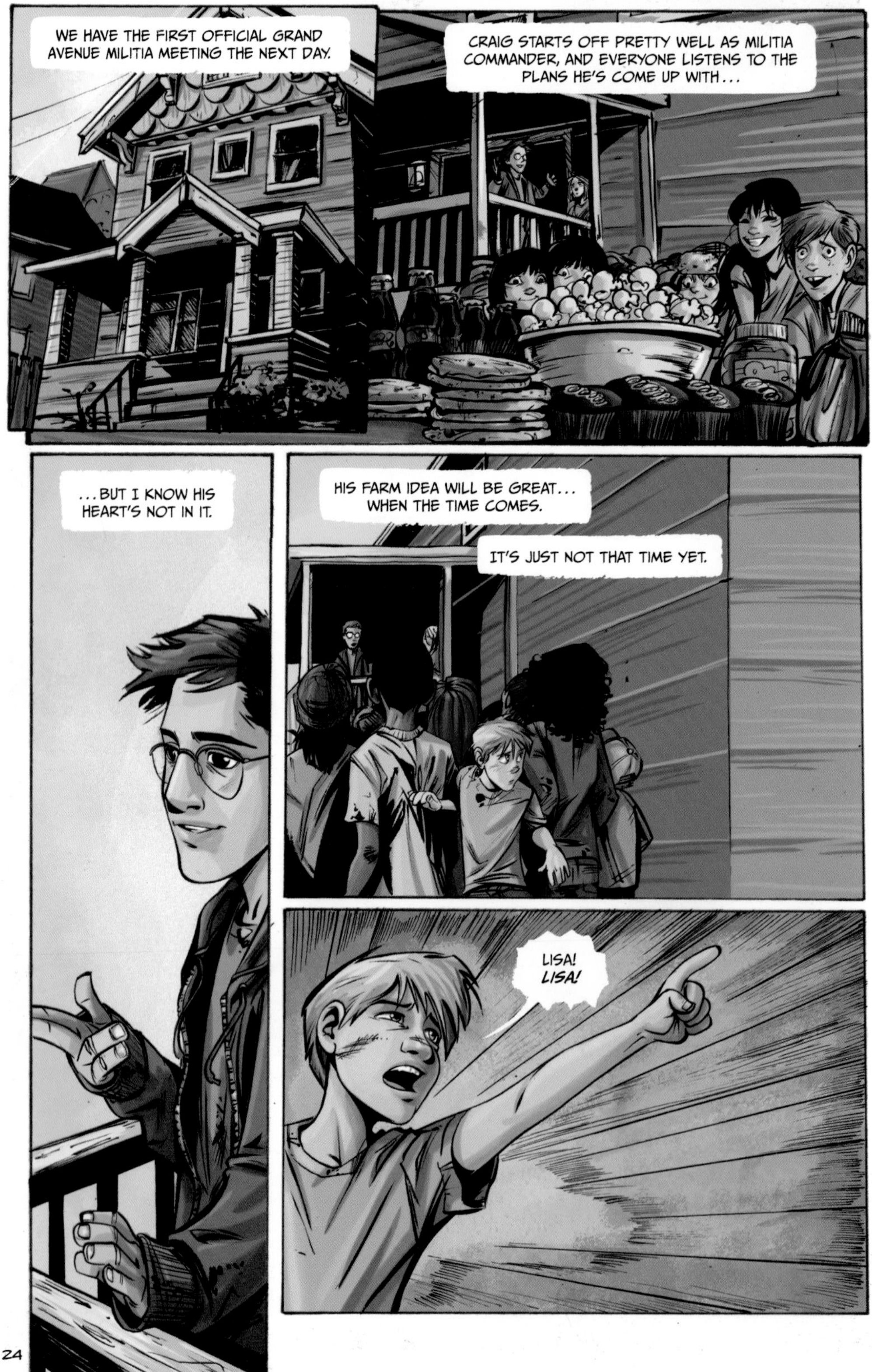
WE HAVE THE FIRST OFFICIAL GRAND AVENUE MILITIA MEETING THE NEXT DAY.
CRAIG STARTS OFF PRETTY WELL AS MILITIA COMMANDER, AND EVERYONE LISTENS TO THE PLANS HE'S COME UP WITH...
...BUT I KNOW HIS HEART'S NOT IN IT.
HIS FARM IDEA WILL BE GREAT... WHEN THE TIME COMES.
IT'S JUST NOT THAT TIME YET.
LISA! *LISA!*

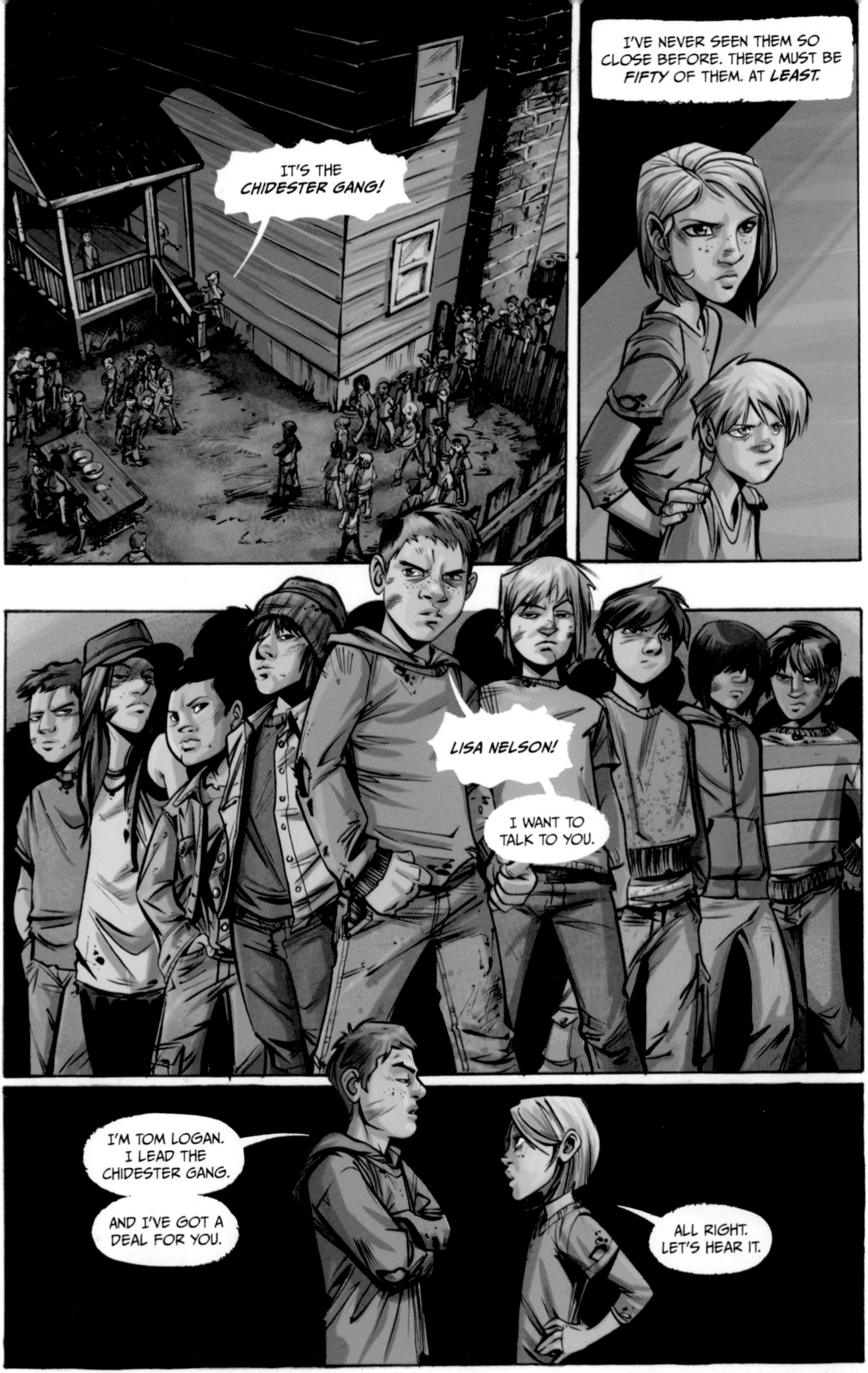
IT'S THE CHIDESTER GANG!
I'VE NEVER SEEN THEM SO CLOSE BEFORE. THERE MUST BE FIFTY OF THEM. AT LEAST.
LISA NELSON!
I WANT TO TALK TO YOU.
I'M TOM LOGAN. I LEAD THE CHIDESTER GANG.
AND I'VE GOT A DEAL FOR YOU.
ALL RIGHT. LET'S HEAR IT.

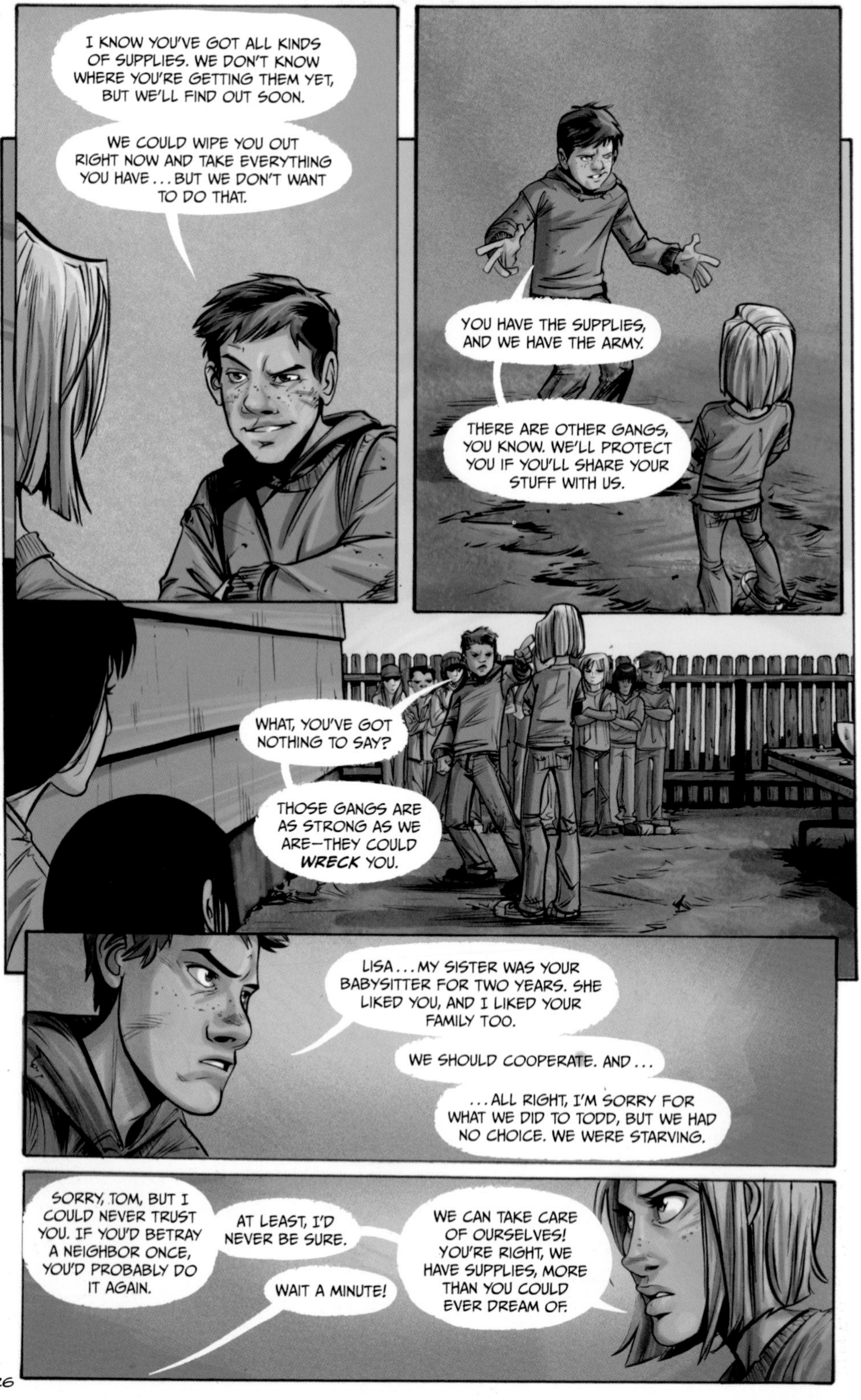
I KNOW YOU'VE GOT ALL KINDS OF SUPPLIES. WE DON'T KNOW WHERE YOU'RE GETTING THEM YET, BUT WE'LL FIND OUT SOON.
WE COULD WIPE YOU OUT RIGHT NOW AND TAKE EVERYTHING YOU HAVE . . . BUT WE DON'T WANT TO DO THAT.
YOU HAVE THE SUPPLIES, AND WE HAVE THE ARMY.
THERE ARE OTHER GANGS, YOU KNOW. WE'LL PROTECT YOU IF YOU'LL SHARE YOUR STUFF WITH US.
WHAT, YOU'VE GOT NOTHING TO SAY?
THOSE GANGS ARE AS STRONG AS WE ARE—THEY COULD *WRECK* YOU.
LISA . . . MY SISTER WAS YOUR BABYSITTER FOR TWO YEARS. SHE LIKED YOU, AND I LIKED YOUR FAMILY TOO.
WE SHOULD COOPERATE. AND . . .
. . . ALL RIGHT, I'M SORRY FOR WHAT WE DID TO TODD, BUT WE HAD NO CHOICE. WE WERE STARVING.
SORRY, TOM, BUT I COULD NEVER TRUST YOU. IF YOU'D BETRAY A NEIGHBOR ONCE, YOU'D PROBABLY DO IT AGAIN.
AT LEAST, I'D NEVER BE SURE.
WAIT A MINUTE!
WE CAN TAKE CARE OF OURSELVES! YOU'RE RIGHT, WE HAVE SUPPLIES, MORE THAN YOU COULD EVER DREAM OF.

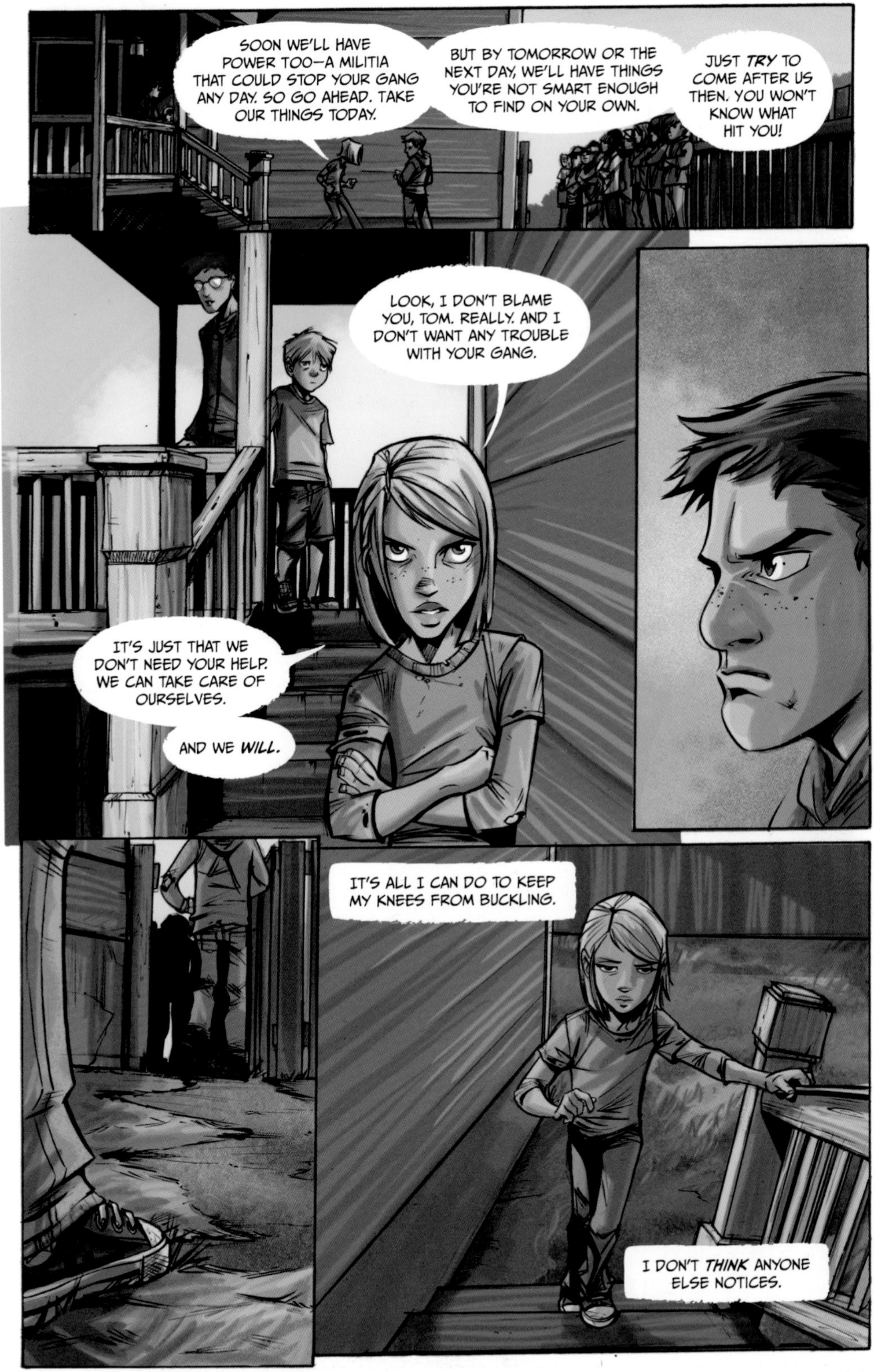
SOON WE'LL HAVE POWER TOO—A MILITIA THAT COULD STOP YOUR GANG ANY DAY. SO GO AHEAD. TAKE OUR THINGS TODAY.
BUT BY TOMORROW OR THE NEXT DAY, WE'LL HAVE THINGS YOU'RE NOT SMART ENOUGH TO FIND ON YOUR OWN.
JUST *TRY* TO COME AFTER US THEN. YOU WON'T KNOW WHAT HIT YOU!
LOOK, I DON'T BLAME YOU, TOM. REALLY. AND I DON'T WANT ANY TROUBLE WITH YOUR GANG.
IT'S JUST THAT WE DON'T NEED YOUR HELP. WE CAN TAKE CARE OF OURSELVES.
AND WE *WILL.*
IT'S ALL I CAN DO TO KEEP MY KNEES FROM BUCKLING.
I DON'T *THINK* ANYONE ELSE NOTICES.

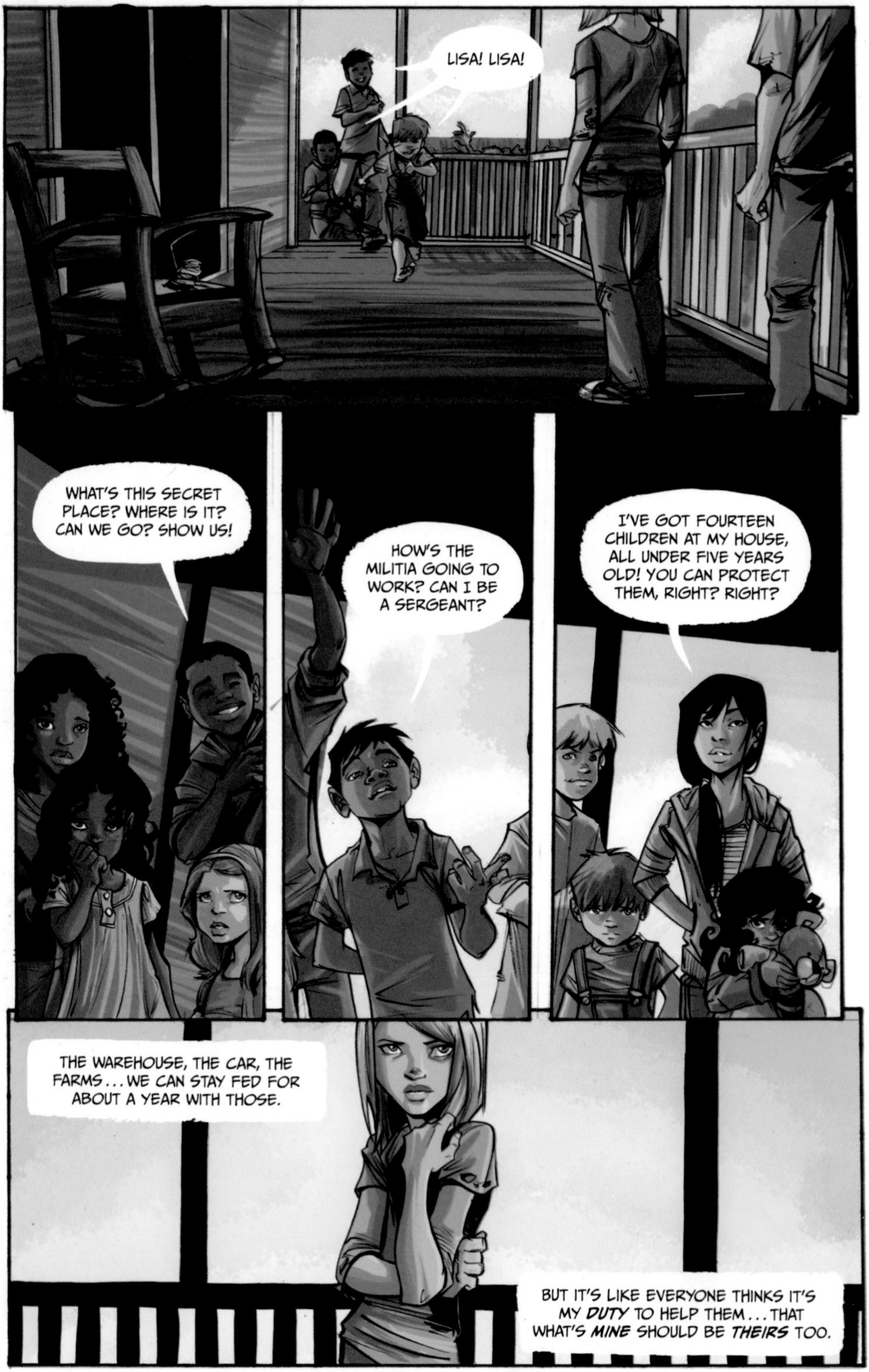
LISA! LISA!
WHAT'S THIS SECRET PLACE? WHERE IS IT? CAN WE GO? SHOW US!
HOW'S THE MILITIA GOING TO WORK? CAN I BE A SERGEANT?
I'VE GOT FOURTEEN CHILDREN AT MY HOUSE, ALL UNDER FIVE YEARS OLD! YOU CAN PROTECT THEM, RIGHT? RIGHT?
THE WAREHOUSE, THE CAR, THE FARMS . . . WE CAN STAY FED FOR ABOUT A YEAR WITH THOSE.
BUT IT'S LIKE EVERYONE THINKS IT'S MY *DUTY* TO HELP THEM . . . THAT WHAT'S *MINE* SHOULD BE *THEIRS* TOO.

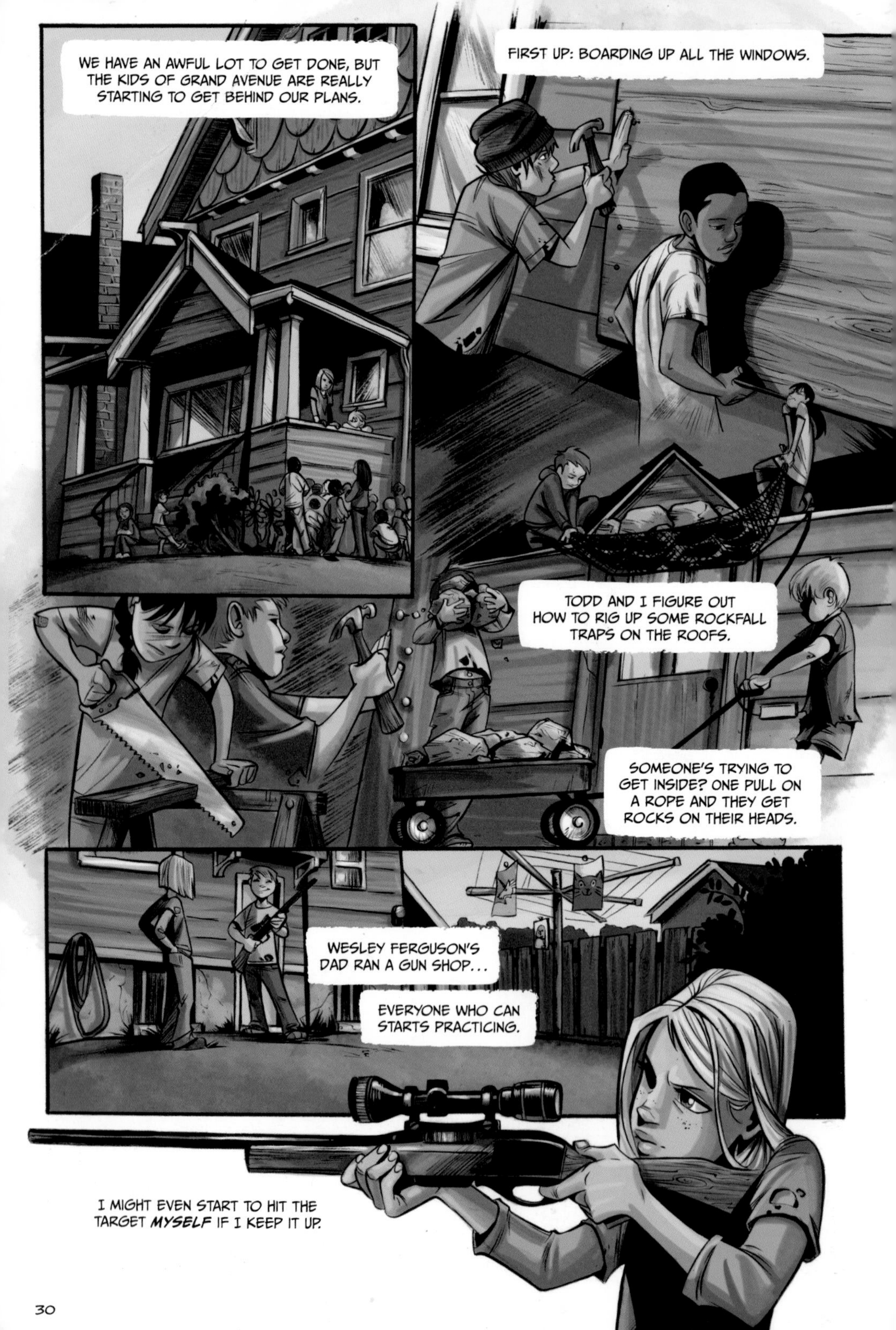
WE HAVE AN AWFUL LOT TO GET DONE, BUT THE KIDS OF GRAND AVENUE ARE REALLY STARTING TO GET BEHIND OUR PLANS.
FIRST UP: BOARDING UP ALL THE WINDOWS.
TODD AND I FIGURE OUT HOW TO RIG UP SOME ROCKFALL TRAPS ON THE ROOFS.
SOMEONE'S TRYING TO GET INSIDE? ONE PULL ON A ROPE AND THEY GET ROCKS ON THEIR HEADS.
WESLEY FERGUSON'S DAD RAN A GUN SHOP...
EVERYONE WHO CAN STARTS PRACTICING.
I MIGHT EVEN START TO HIT THE TARGET ***MYSELF*** IF I KEEP IT UP.

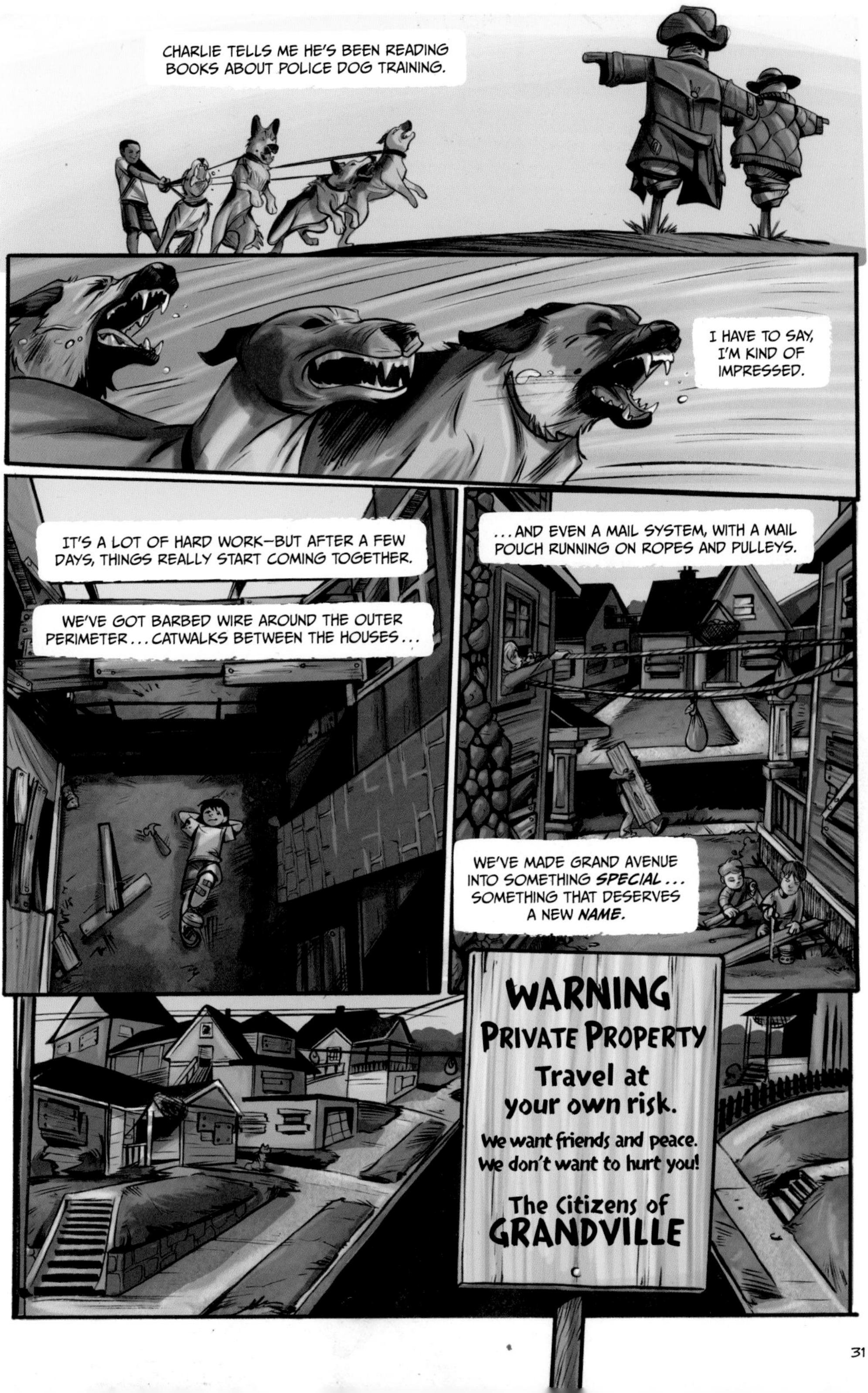
CHARLIE TELLS ME HE'S BEEN READING BOOKS ABOUT POLICE DOG TRAINING.
I HAVE TO SAY, I'M KIND OF IMPRESSED.
IT'S A LOT OF HARD WORK—BUT AFTER A FEW DAYS, THINGS REALLY START COMING TOGETHER.
WE'VE GOT BARBED WIRE AROUND THE OUTER PERIMETER . . . CATWALKS BETWEEN THE HOUSES . . .
. . . AND EVEN A MAIL SYSTEM, WITH A MAIL POUCH RUNNING ON ROPES AND PULLEYS.
WE'VE MADE GRAND AVENUE INTO SOMETHING *SPECIAL* . . . SOMETHING THAT DESERVES A NEW *NAME*.
WARNING
PRIVATE PROPERTY
Travel at your own risk.
We want friends and peace. We don't want to hurt you!
The Citizens of GRANDVILLE

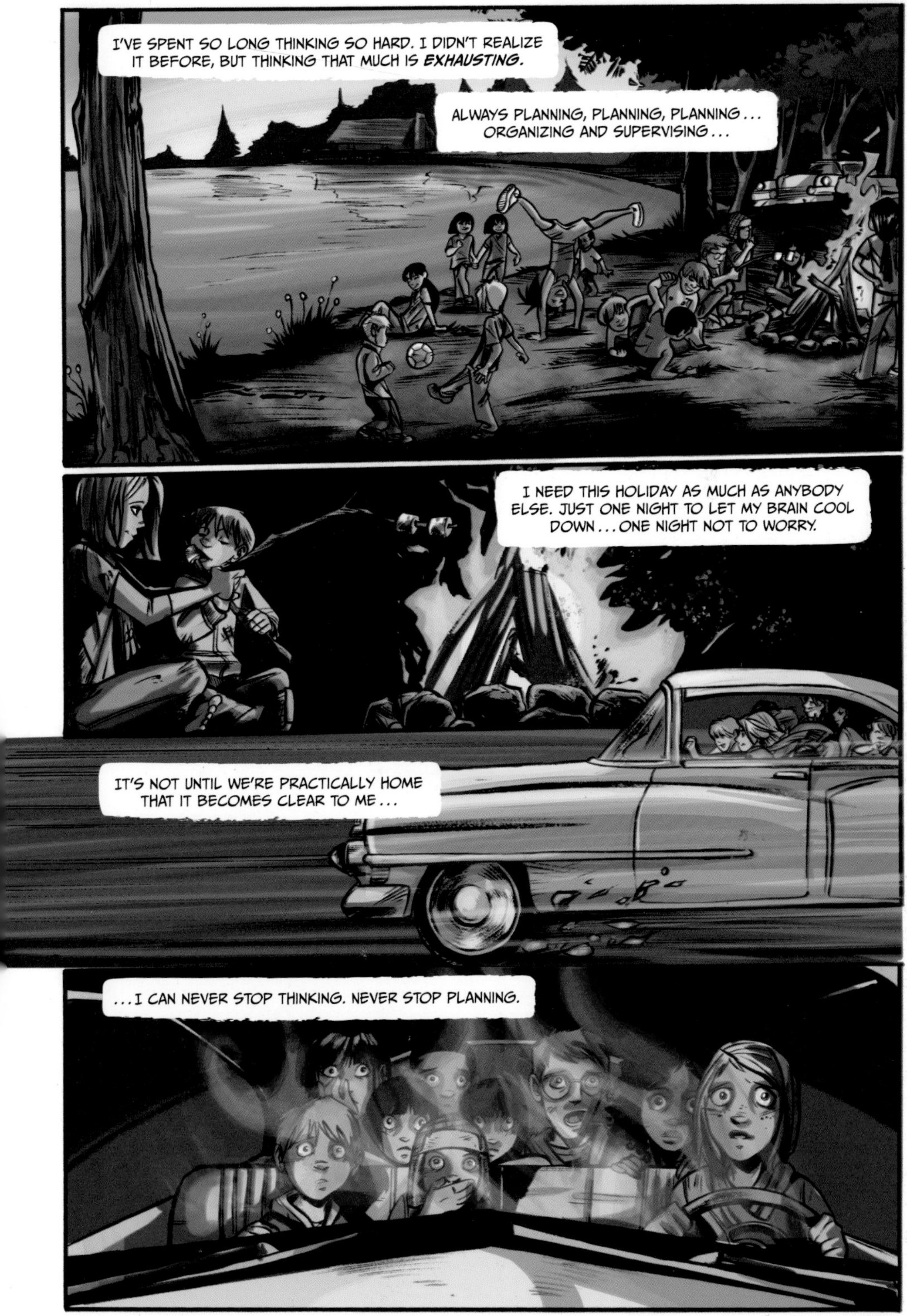
I'VE SPENT SO LONG THINKING SO HARD. I DIDN'T REALIZE IT BEFORE, BUT THINKING THAT MUCH IS *EXHAUSTING.*
ALWAYS PLANNING, PLANNING, PLANNING . . . ORGANIZING AND SUPERVISING . . .
I NEED THIS HOLIDAY AS MUCH AS ANYBODY ELSE. JUST ONE NIGHT TO LET MY BRAIN COOL DOWN . . . ONE NIGHT NOT TO WORRY.
IT'S NOT UNTIL WE'RE PRACTICALLY HOME THAT IT BECOMES CLEAR TO ME . . .
. . . I CAN NEVER STOP THINKING. NEVER STOP PLANNING.

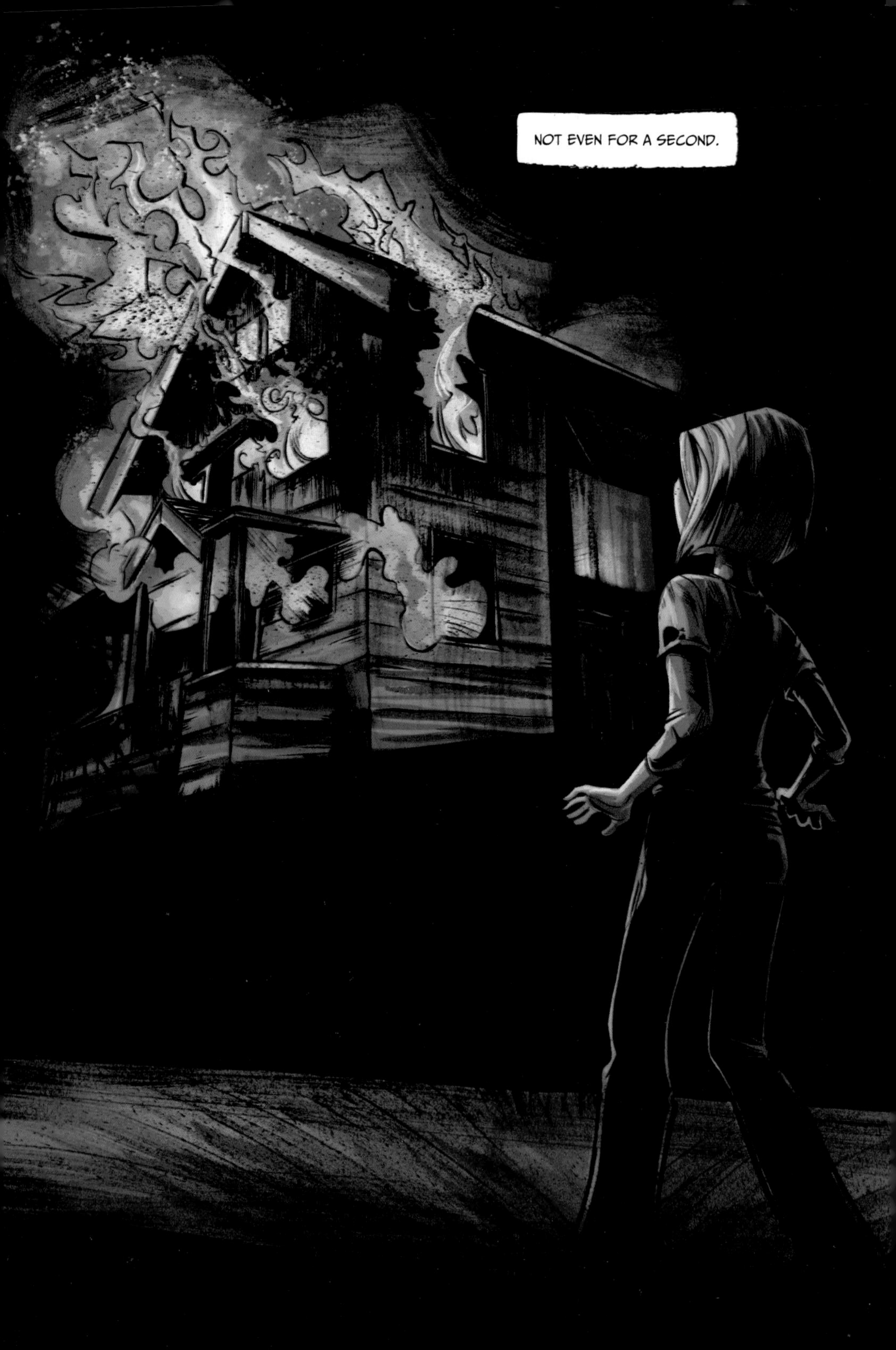
NOT EVEN FOR A SECOND.

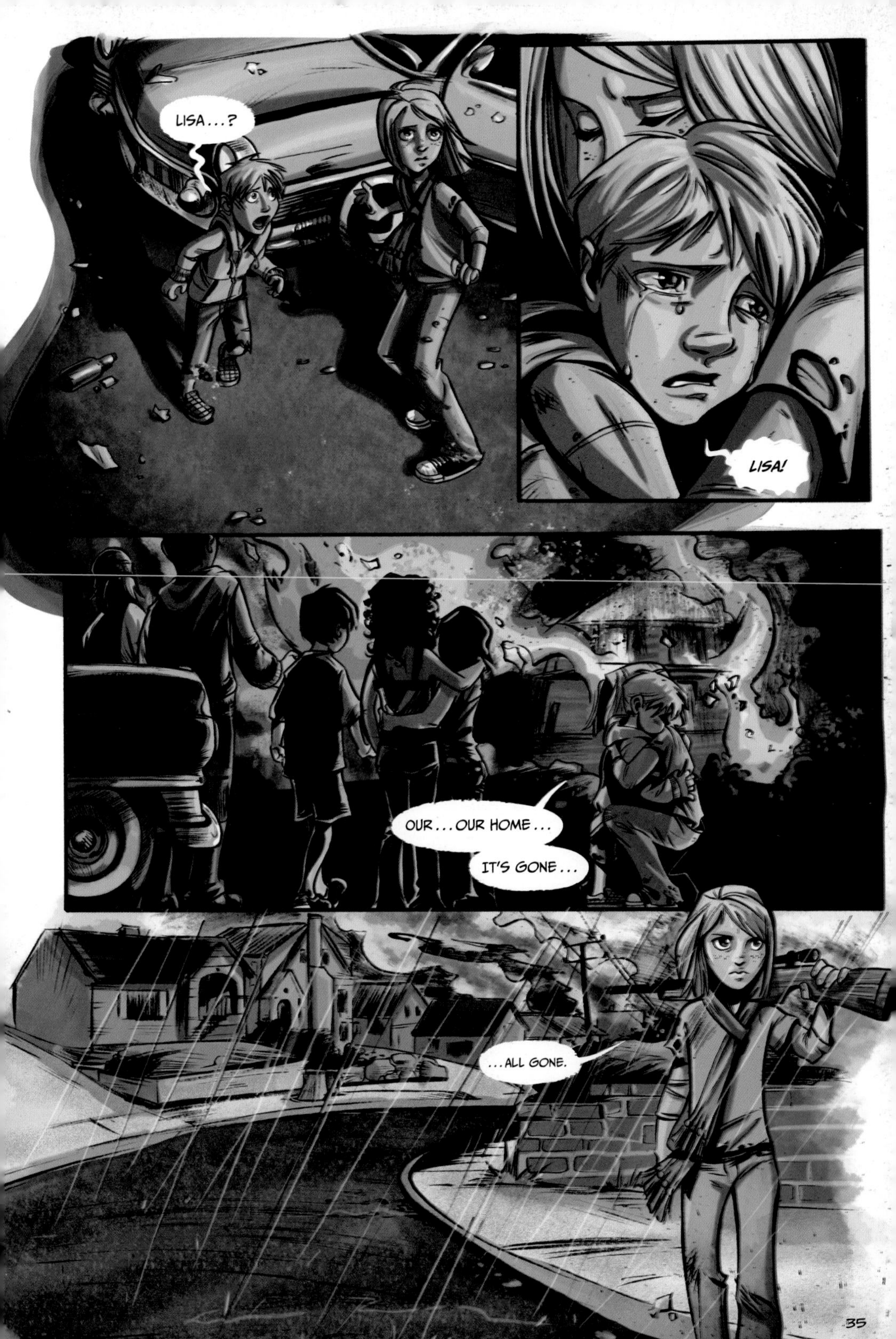
LISA...?
LISA!
OUR...OUR HOME...
IT'S GONE...
...ALL GONE.

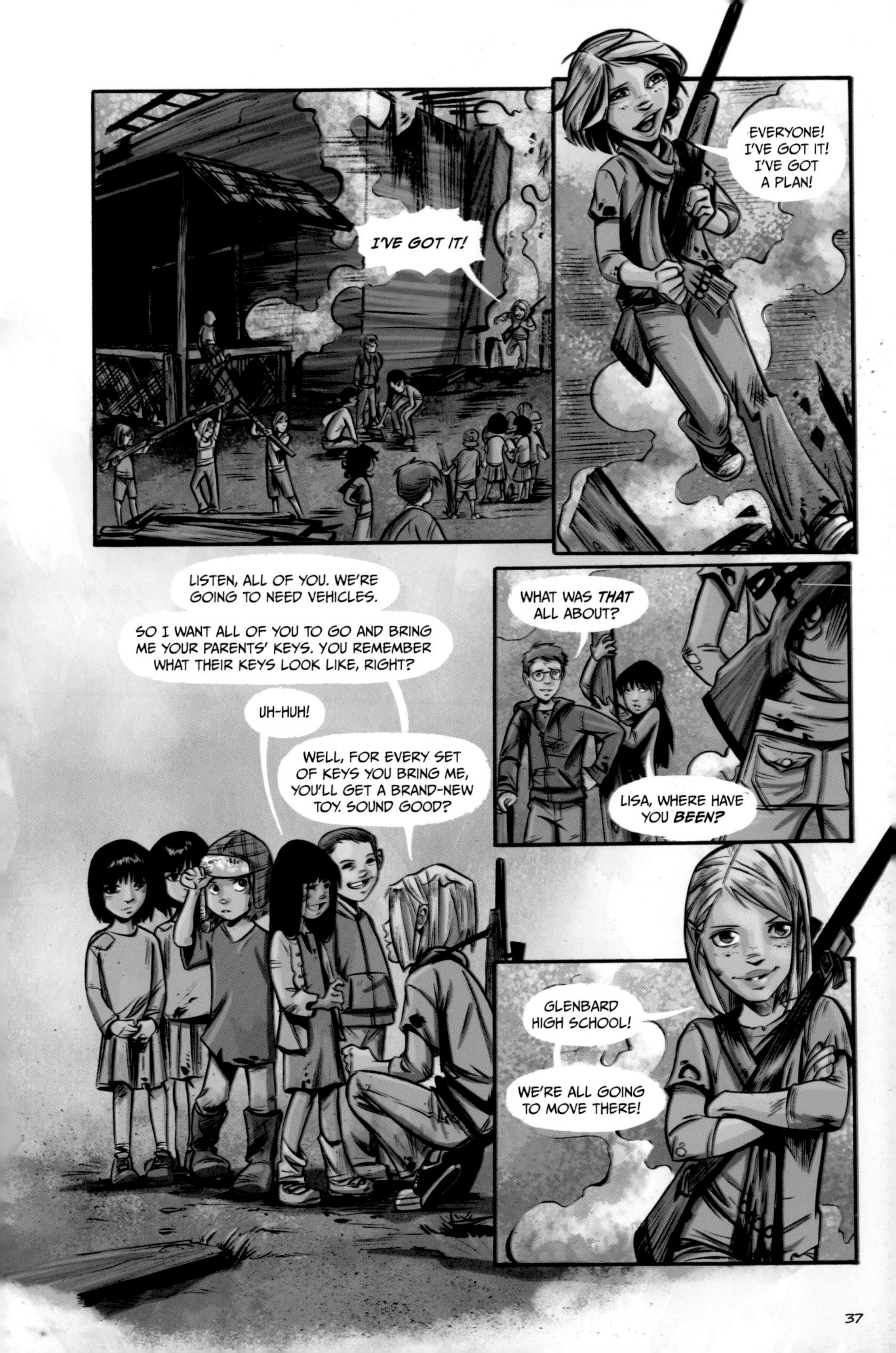
I'VE GOT IT!
EVERYONE! I'VE GOT IT! I'VE GOT A PLAN!
LISTEN, ALL OF YOU. WE'RE GOING TO NEED VEHICLES.
SO I WANT ALL OF YOU TO GO AND BRING ME YOUR PARENTS' KEYS. YOU REMEMBER WHAT THEIR KEYS LOOK LIKE, RIGHT?
UH-HUH!
WELL, FOR EVERY SET OF KEYS YOU BRING ME, YOU'LL GET A BRAND-NEW TOY. SOUND GOOD?
WHAT WAS *THAT* ALL ABOUT?
LISA, WHERE HAVE YOU ***BEEN?***
GLENBARD HIGH SCHOOL!
WE'RE ALL GOING TO MOVE THERE!

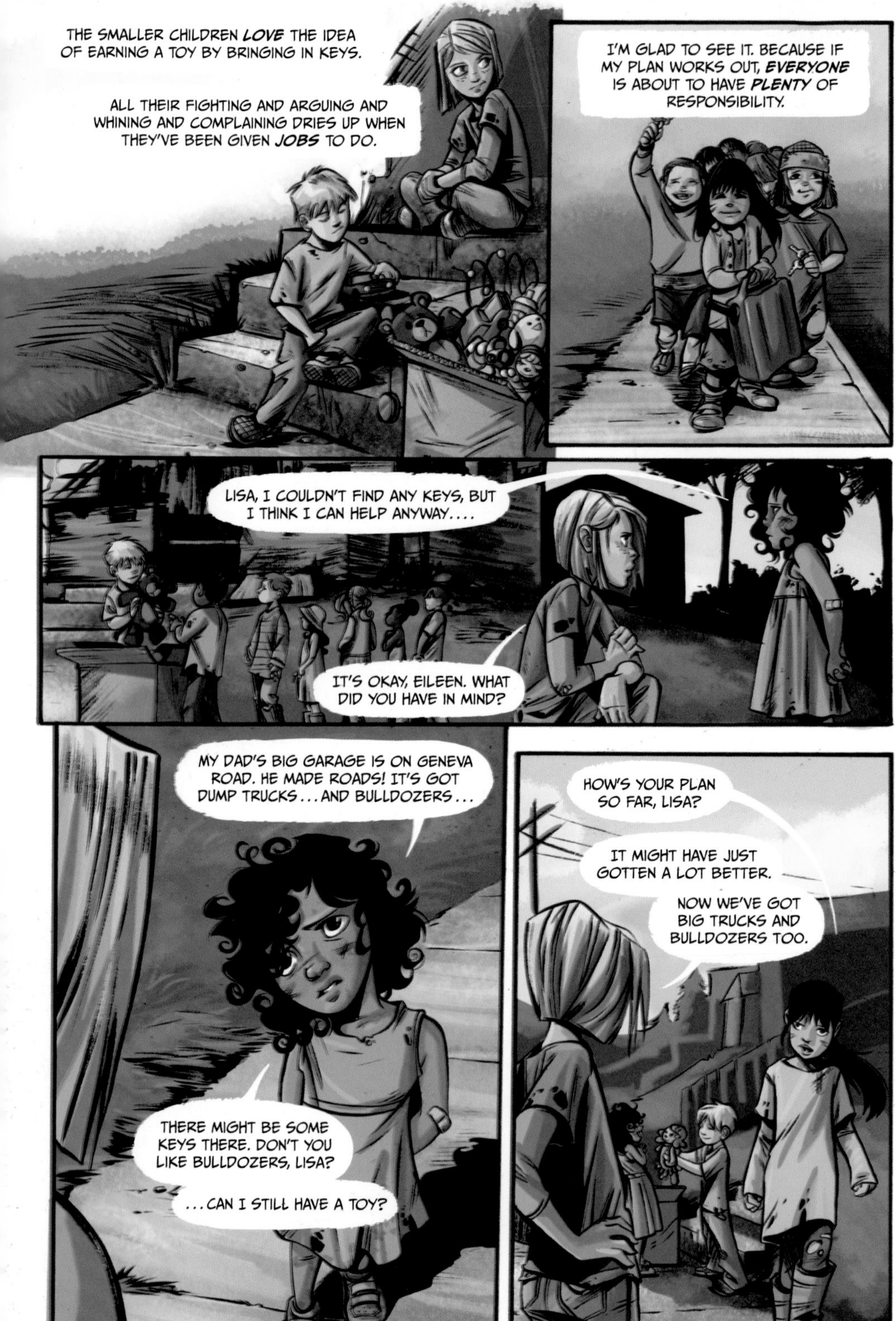
THE SMALLER CHILDREN LOVE THE IDEA OF EARNING A TOY BY BRINGING IN KEYS.
ALL THEIR FIGHTING AND ARGUING AND WHINING AND COMPLAINING DRIES UP WHEN THEY'VE BEEN GIVEN JOBS TO DO.
I'M GLAD TO SEE IT. BECAUSE IF MY PLAN WORKS OUT, EVERYONE IS ABOUT TO HAVE PLENTY OF RESPONSIBILITY.
LISA, I COULDN'T FIND ANY KEYS, BUT I THINK I CAN HELP ANYWAY....
IT'S OKAY, EILEEN. WHAT DID YOU HAVE IN MIND?
MY DAD'S BIG GARAGE IS ON GENEVA ROAD. HE MADE ROADS! IT'S GOT DUMP TRUCKS... AND BULLDOZERS...
THERE MIGHT BE SOME KEYS THERE. DON'T YOU LIKE BULLDOZERS, LISA?
...CAN I STILL HAVE A TOY?
HOW'S YOUR PLAN SO FAR, LISA?
IT MIGHT HAVE JUST GOTTEN A LOT BETTER.
NOW WE'VE GOT BIG TRUCKS AND BULLDOZERS TOO.

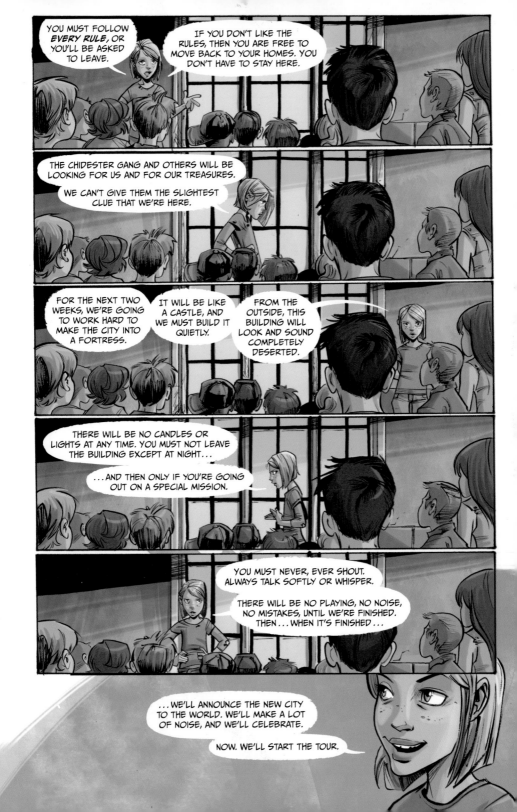

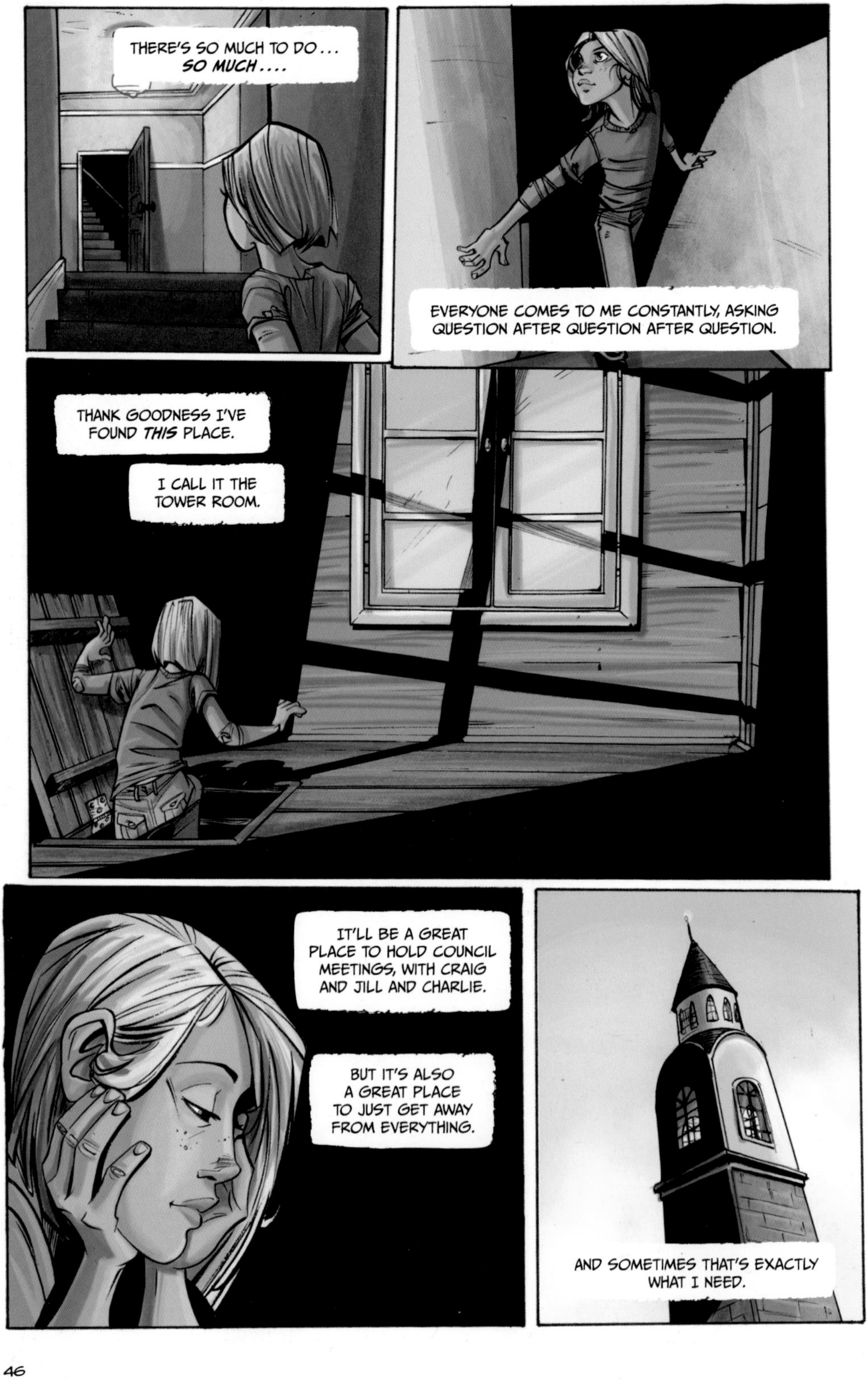
THERE'S SO MUCH TO DO . . .
SO MUCH . . . .
EVERYONE COMES TO ME CONSTANTLY, ASKING QUESTION AFTER QUESTION AFTER QUESTION.
THANK GOODNESS I'VE FOUND *THIS* PLACE.
I CALL IT THE TOWER ROOM.
IT'LL BE A GREAT PLACE TO HOLD COUNCIL MEETINGS, WITH CRAIG AND JILL AND CHARLIE.
BUT IT'S ALSO A GREAT PLACE TO JUST GET AWAY FROM EVERYTHING.
AND SOMETIMES THAT'S EXACTLY WHAT I NEED.

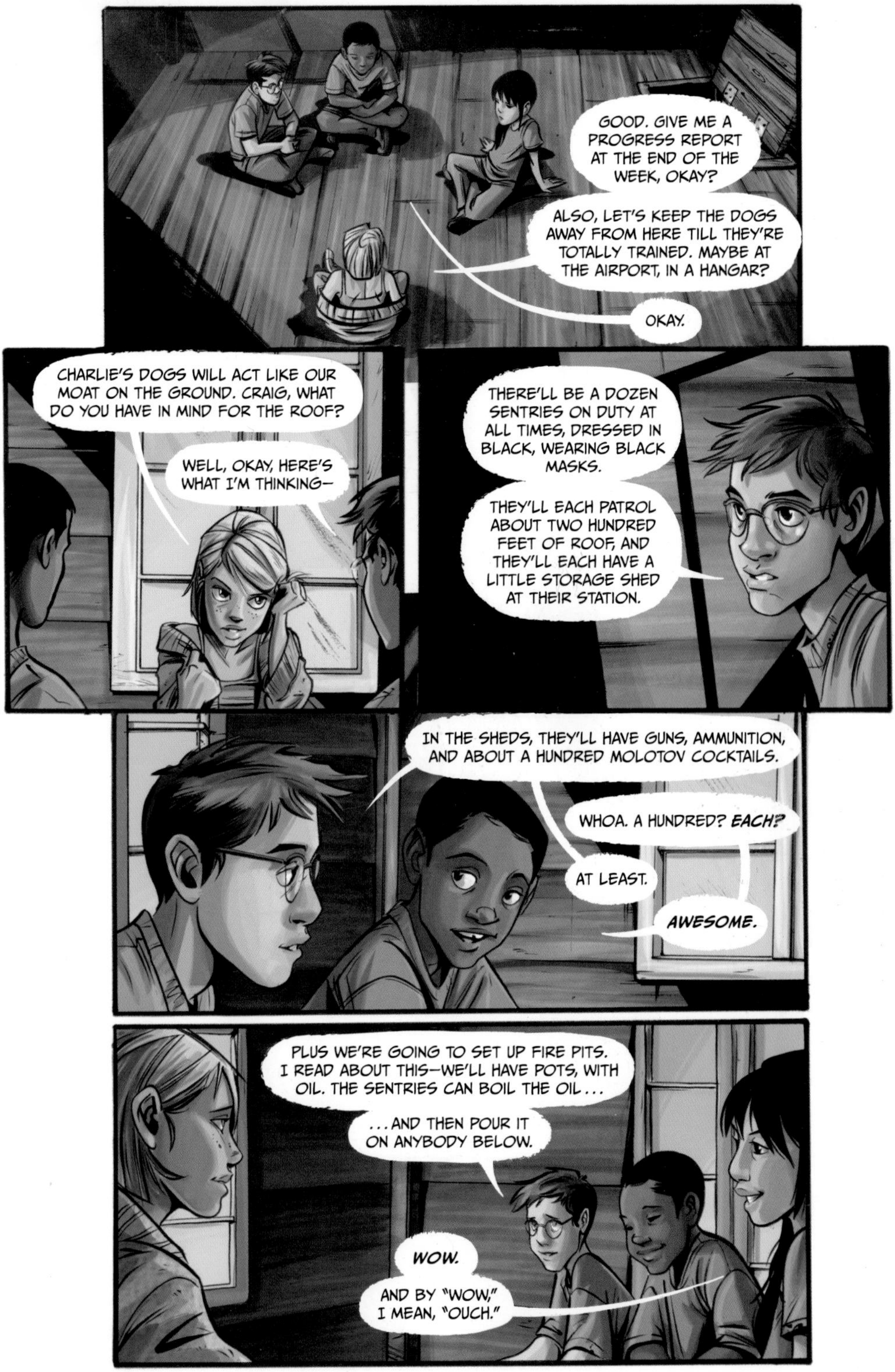
GOOD. GIVE ME A PROGRESS REPORT AT THE END OF THE WEEK, OKAY?
ALSO, LET'S KEEP THE DOGS AWAY FROM HERE TILL THEY'RE TOTALLY TRAINED. MAYBE AT THE AIRPORT, IN A HANGAR?
OKAY.
CHARLIE'S DOGS WILL ACT LIKE OUR MOAT ON THE GROUND. CRAIG, WHAT DO YOU HAVE IN MIND FOR THE ROOF?
WELL, OKAY, HERE'S WHAT I'M THINKING—
THERE'LL BE A DOZEN SENTRIES ON DUTY AT ALL TIMES, DRESSED IN BLACK, WEARING BLACK MASKS.
THEY'LL EACH PATROL ABOUT TWO HUNDRED FEET OF ROOF, AND THEY'LL EACH HAVE A LITTLE STORAGE SHED AT THEIR STATION.
IN THE SHEDS, THEY'LL HAVE GUNS, AMMUNITION, AND ABOUT A HUNDRED MOLOTOV COCKTAILS.
WHOA. A HUNDRED? EACH?
AT LEAST.
AWESOME.
PLUS WE'RE GOING TO SET UP FIRE PITS. I READ ABOUT THIS—WE'LL HAVE POTS, WITH OIL. THE SENTRIES CAN BOIL THE OIL . . .
. . . AND THEN POUR IT ON ANYBODY BELOW.
WOW.
AND BY "WOW," I MEAN, "OUCH."

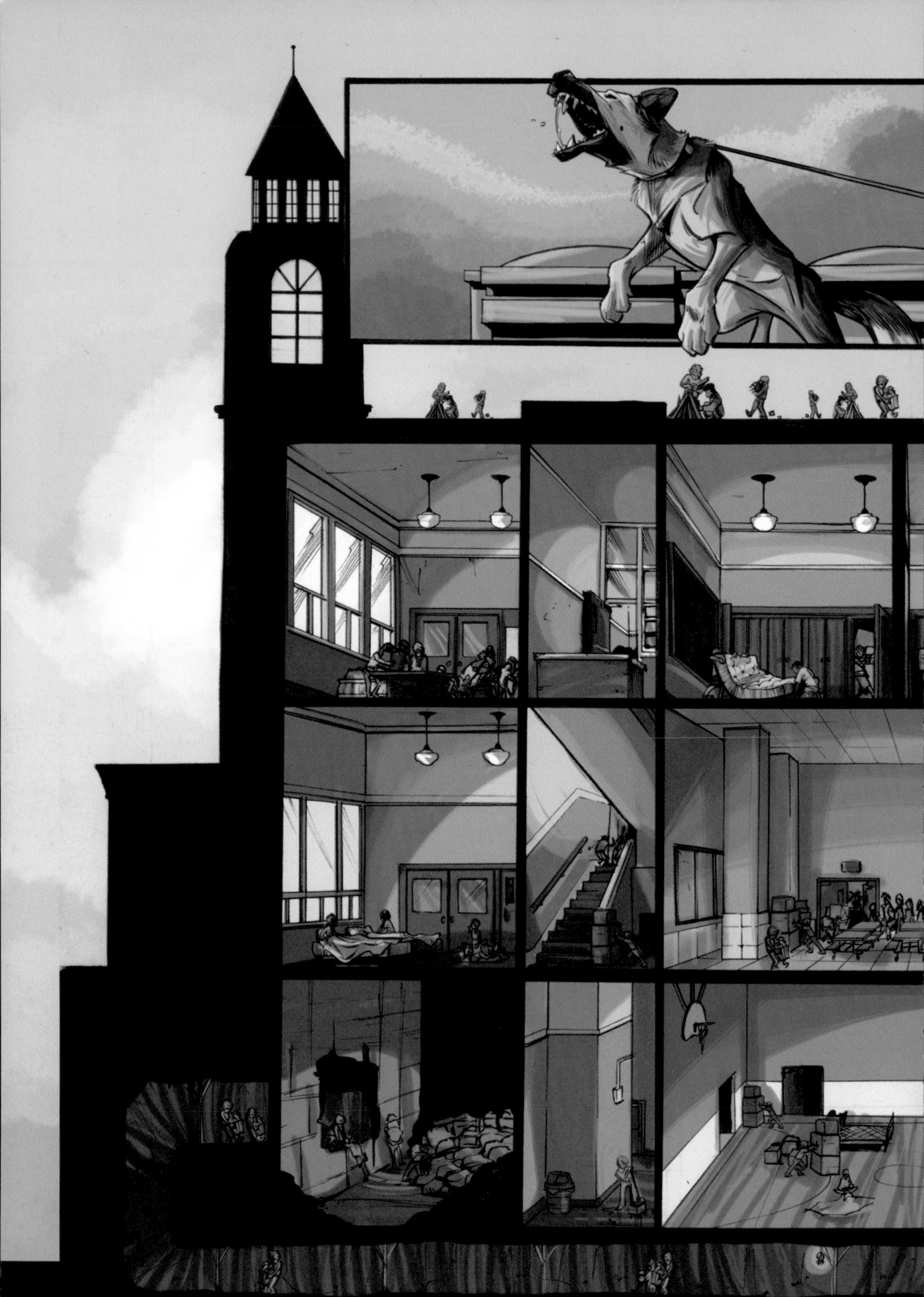

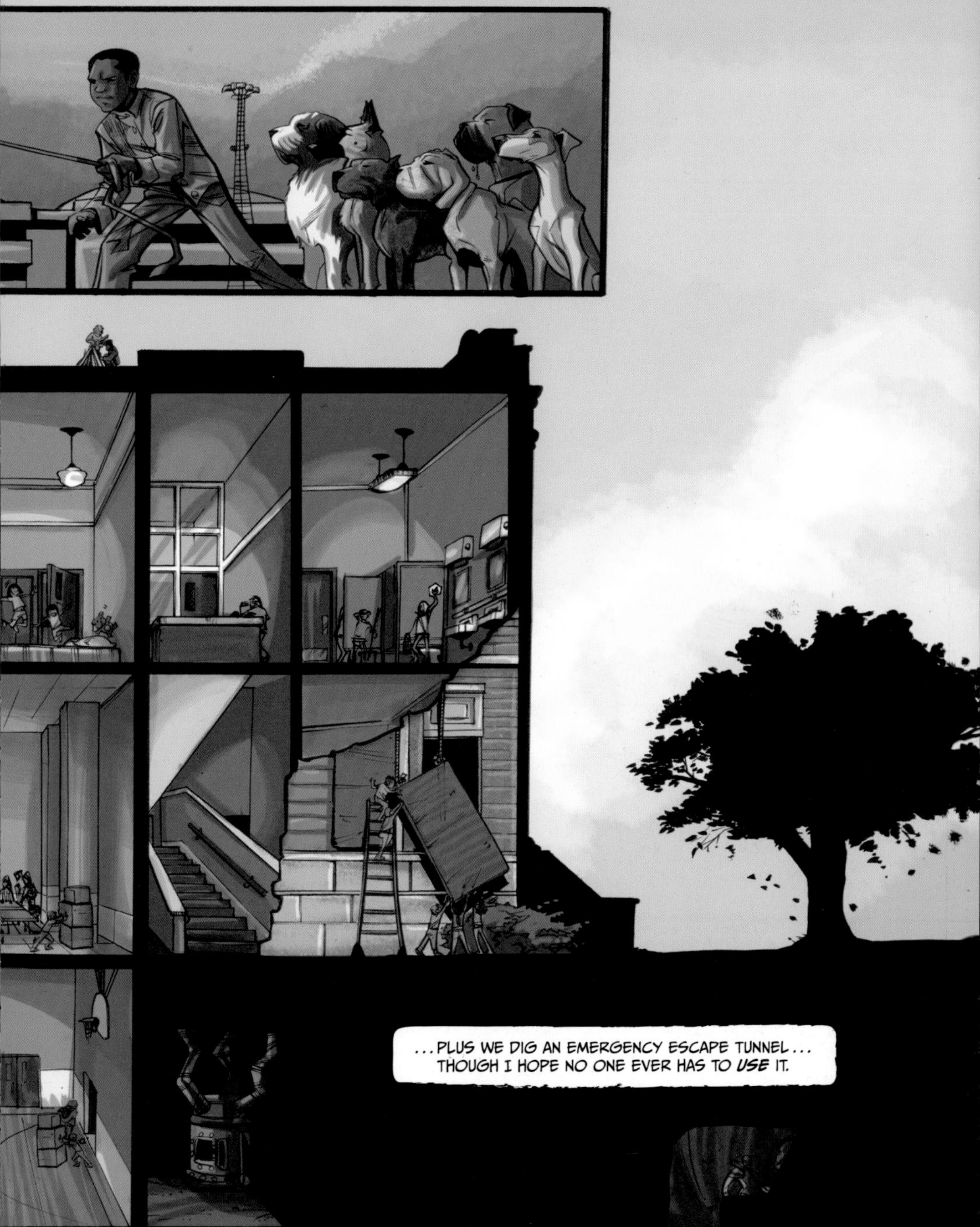
...PLUS WE DIG AN EMERGENCY ESCAPE TUNNEL...
THOUGH I HOPE NO ONE EVER HAS TO USE IT.

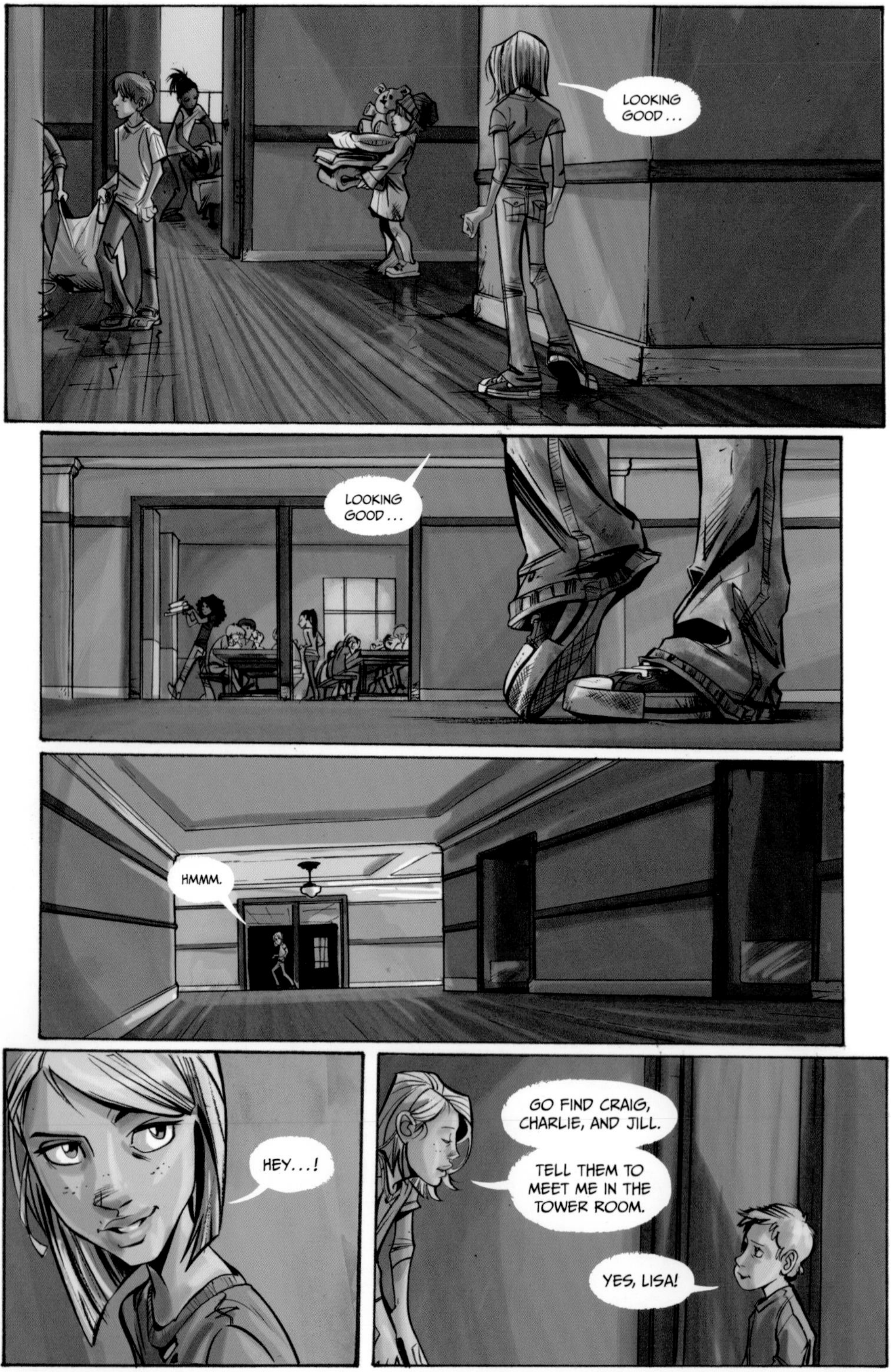
LOOKING GOOD...
LOOKING GOOD...
HMMM.
HEY...!
GO FIND CRAIG, CHARLIE, AND JILL.
TELL THEM TO MEET ME IN THE TOWER ROOM.
YES, LISA!

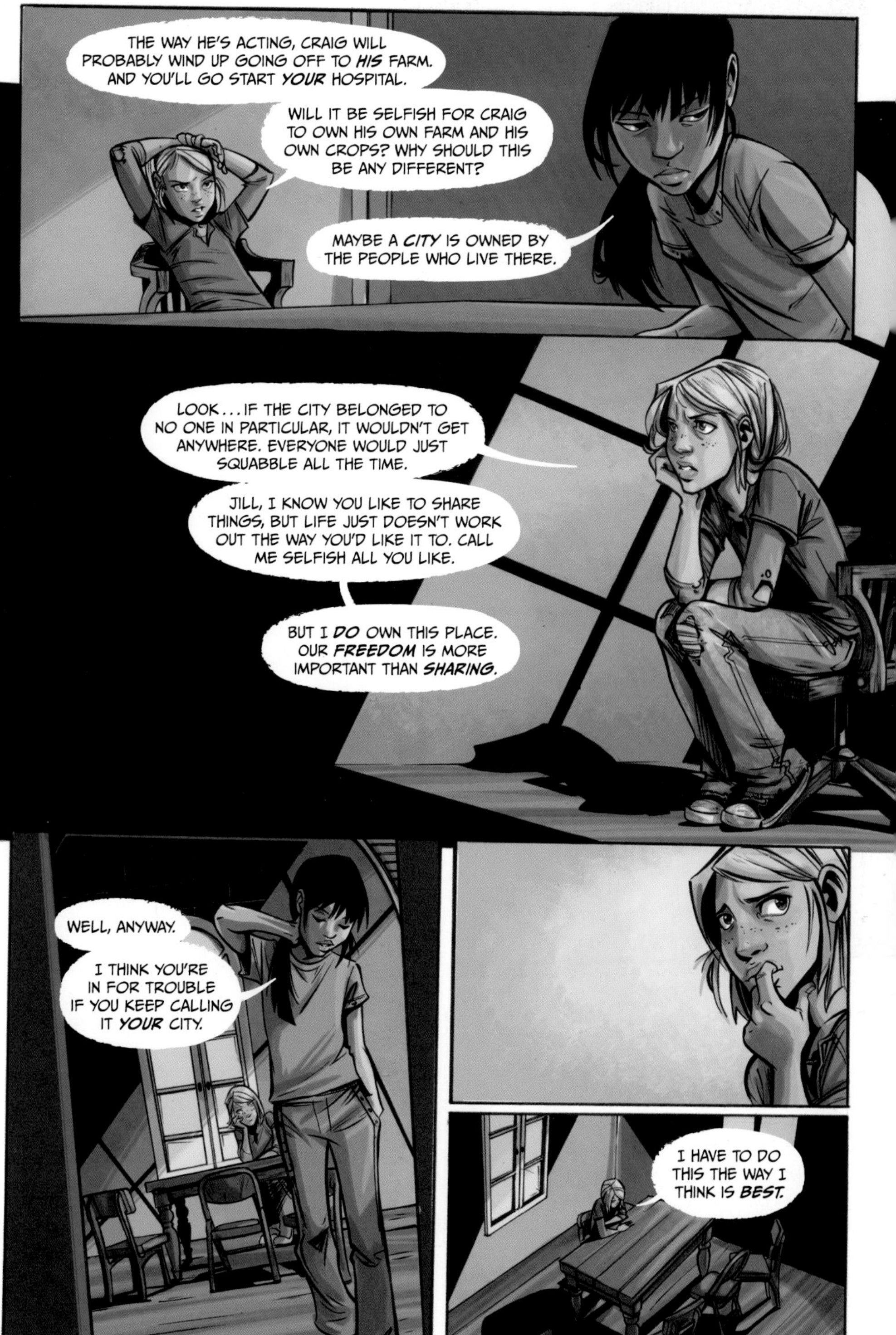
THE WAY HE'S ACTING, CRAIG WILL PROBABLY WIND UP GOING OFF TO *HIS* FARM. AND YOU'LL GO START *YOUR* HOSPITAL.
WILL IT BE SELFISH FOR CRAIG TO OWN HIS OWN FARM AND HIS OWN CROPS? WHY SHOULD THIS BE ANY DIFFERENT?
MAYBE A *CITY* IS OWNED BY THE PEOPLE WHO LIVE THERE.
LOOK . . . IF THE CITY BELONGED TO NO ONE IN PARTICULAR, IT WOULDN'T GET ANYWHERE. EVERYONE WOULD JUST SQUABBLE ALL THE TIME.
JILL, I KNOW YOU LIKE TO SHARE THINGS, BUT LIFE JUST DOESN'T WORK OUT THE WAY YOU'D LIKE IT TO. CALL ME SELFISH ALL YOU LIKE.
BUT I *DO* OWN THIS PLACE. OUR *FREEDOM* IS MORE IMPORTANT THAN *SHARING*.
WELL, ANYWAY.
I THINK YOU'RE IN FOR TROUBLE IF YOU KEEP CALLING IT *YOUR* CITY.
I HAVE TO DO THIS THE WAY I THINK IS *BEST*.

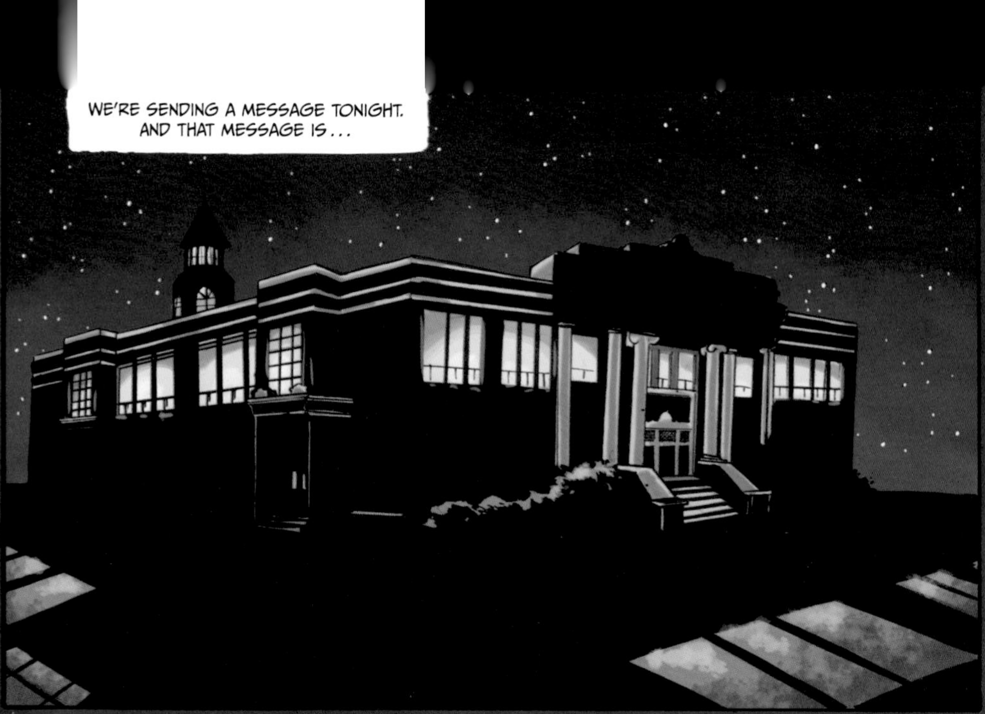
WE'RE SENDING A MESSAGE TONIGHT. AND THAT MESSAGE IS . . .

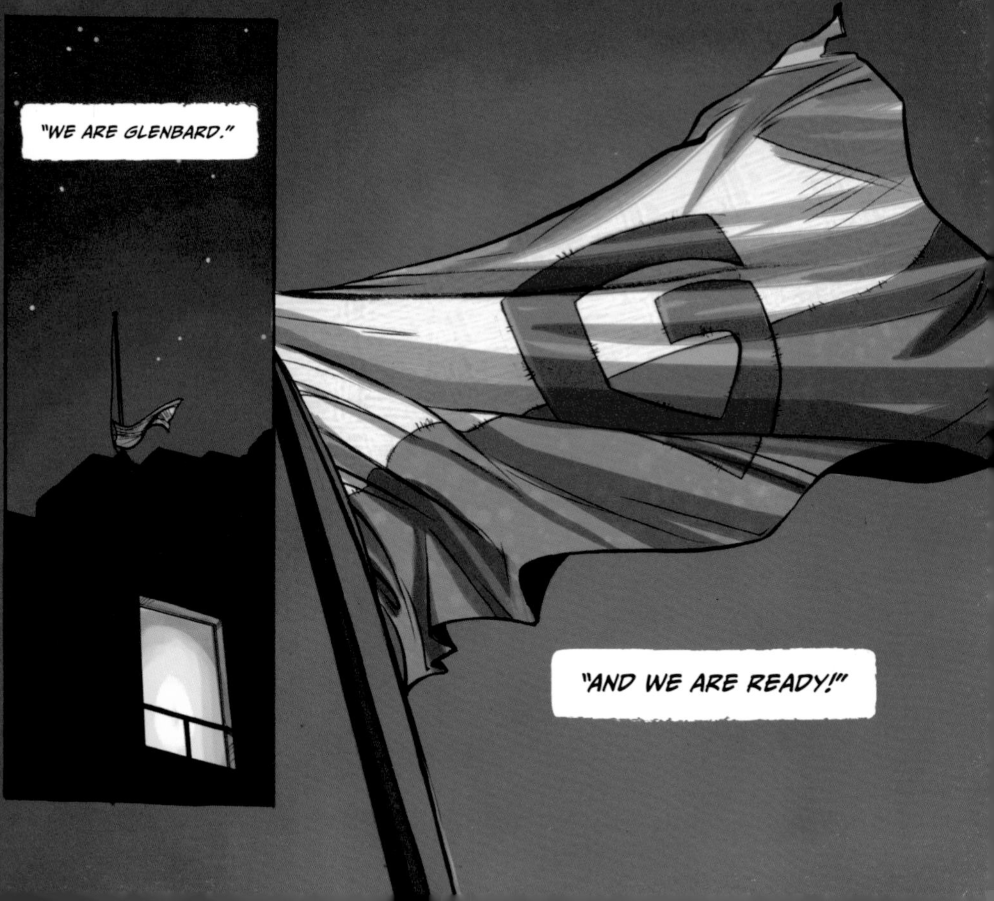
"WE ARE GLENBARD."
"AND WE ARE READY!"

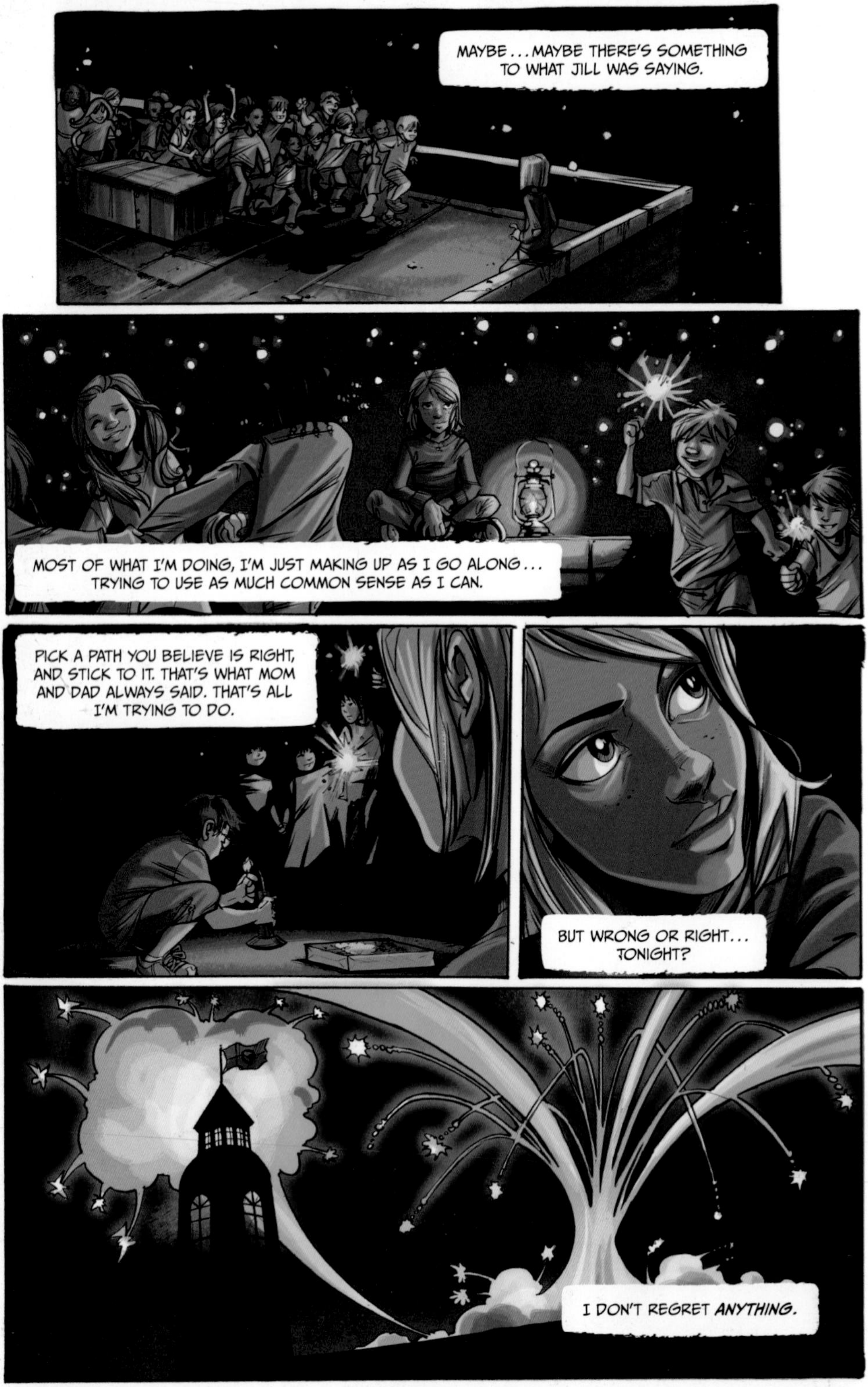
MAYBE . . . MAYBE THERE'S SOMETHING TO WHAT JILL WAS SAYING.
MOST OF WHAT I'M DOING, I'M JUST MAKING UP AS I GO ALONG . . . TRYING TO USE AS MUCH COMMON SENSE AS I CAN.
PICK A PATH YOU BELIEVE IS RIGHT, AND STICK TO IT. THAT'S WHAT MOM AND DAD ALWAYS SAID. THAT'S ALL I'M TRYING TO DO.
BUT WRONG OR RIGHT . . . TONIGHT?
I DON'T REGRET *ANYTHING.*

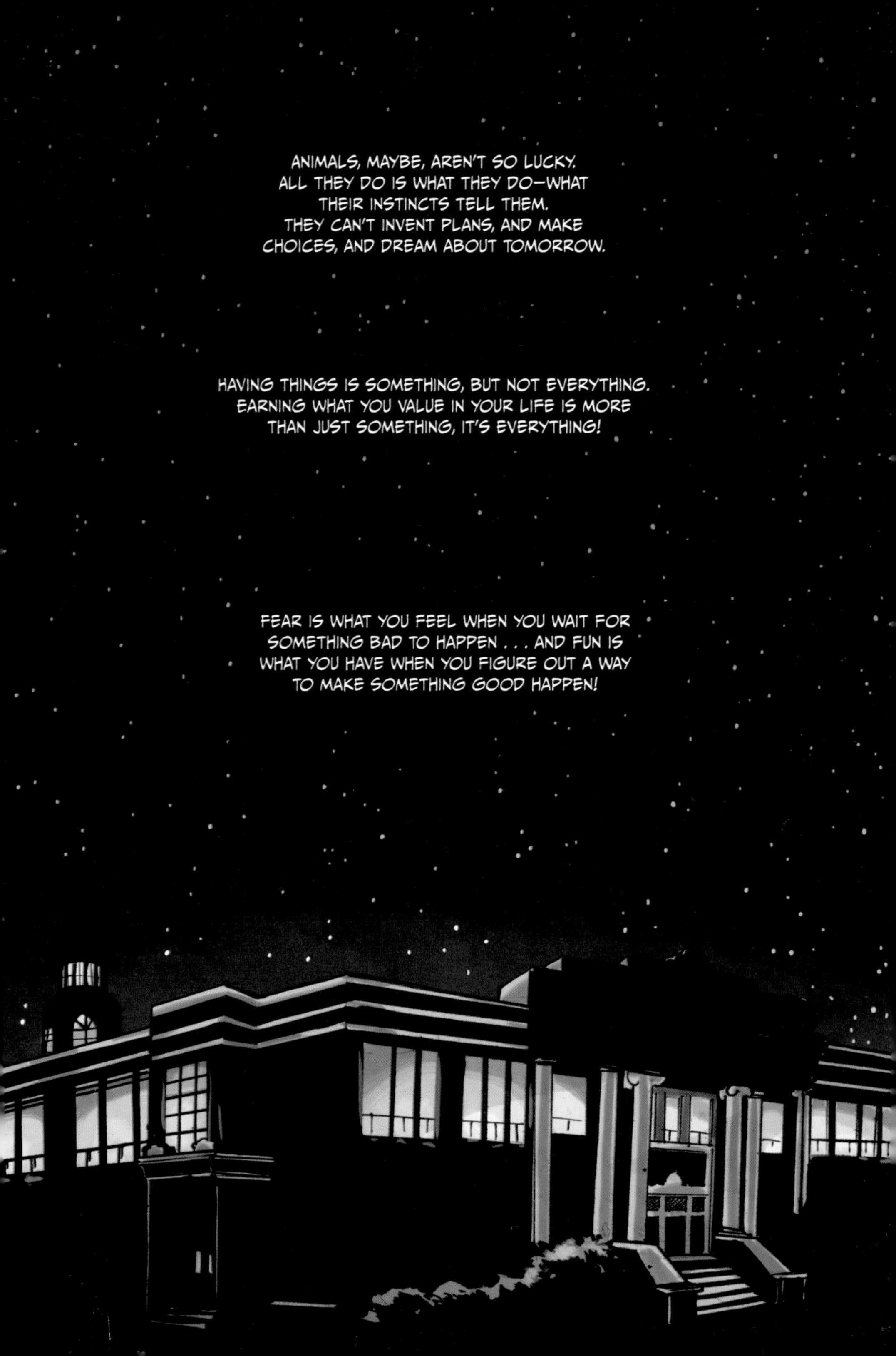
ANIMALS, MAYBE, AREN'T SO LUCKY. ALL THEY DO IS WHAT THEY DO—WHAT THEIR INSTINCTS TELL THEM. THEY CAN'T INVENT PLANS, AND MAKE CHOICES, AND DREAM ABOUT TOMORROW.
HAVING THINGS IS SOMETHING, BUT NOT EVERYTHING. EARNING WHAT YOU VALUE IN YOUR LIFE IS MORE THAN JUST SOMETHING, IT'S EVERYTHING!
FEAR IS WHAT YOU FEEL WHEN YOU WAIT FOR SOMETHING BAD TO HAPPEN . . . AND FUN IS WHAT YOU HAVE WHEN YOU FIGURE OUT A WAY TO MAKE SOMETHING GOOD HAPPEN!

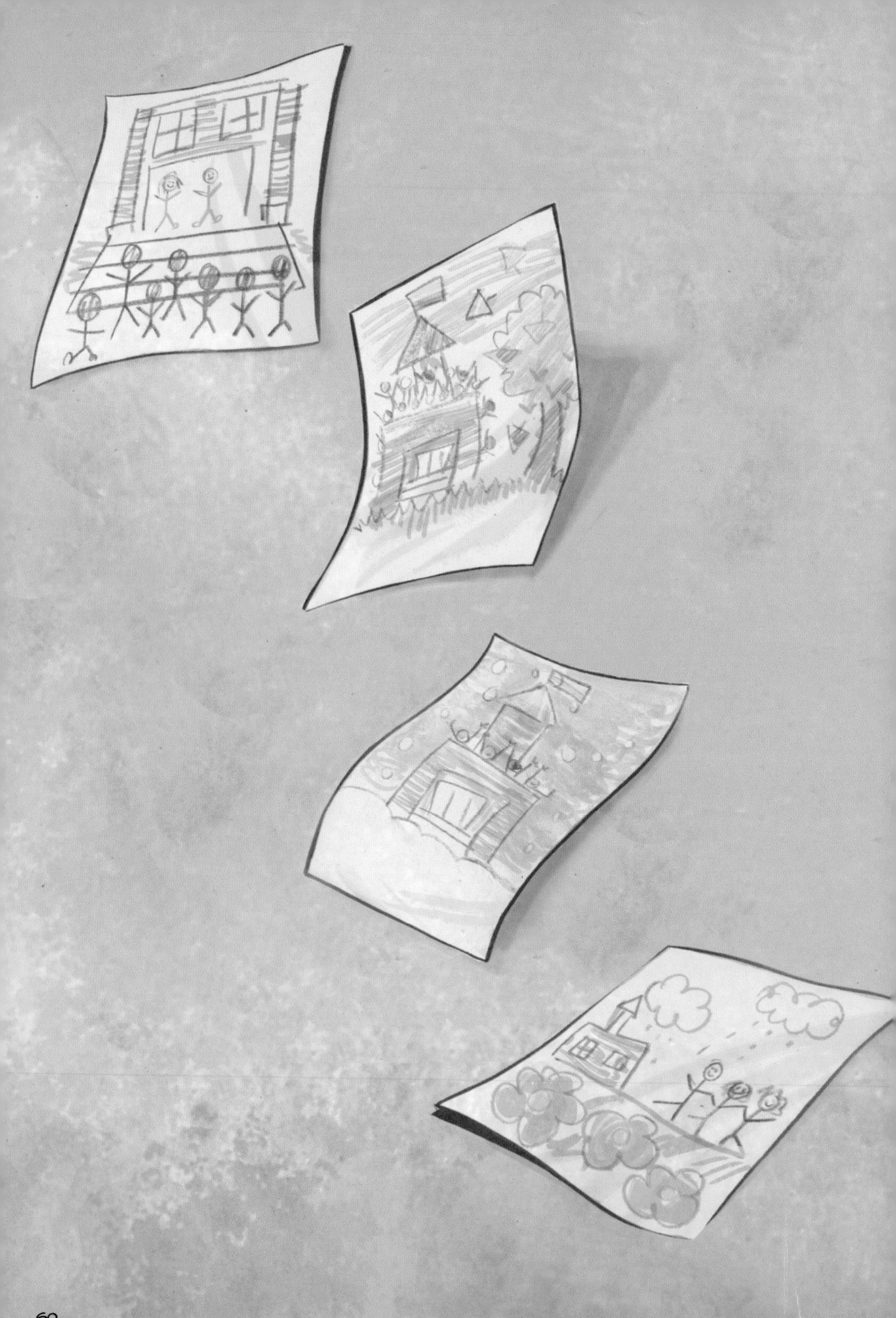

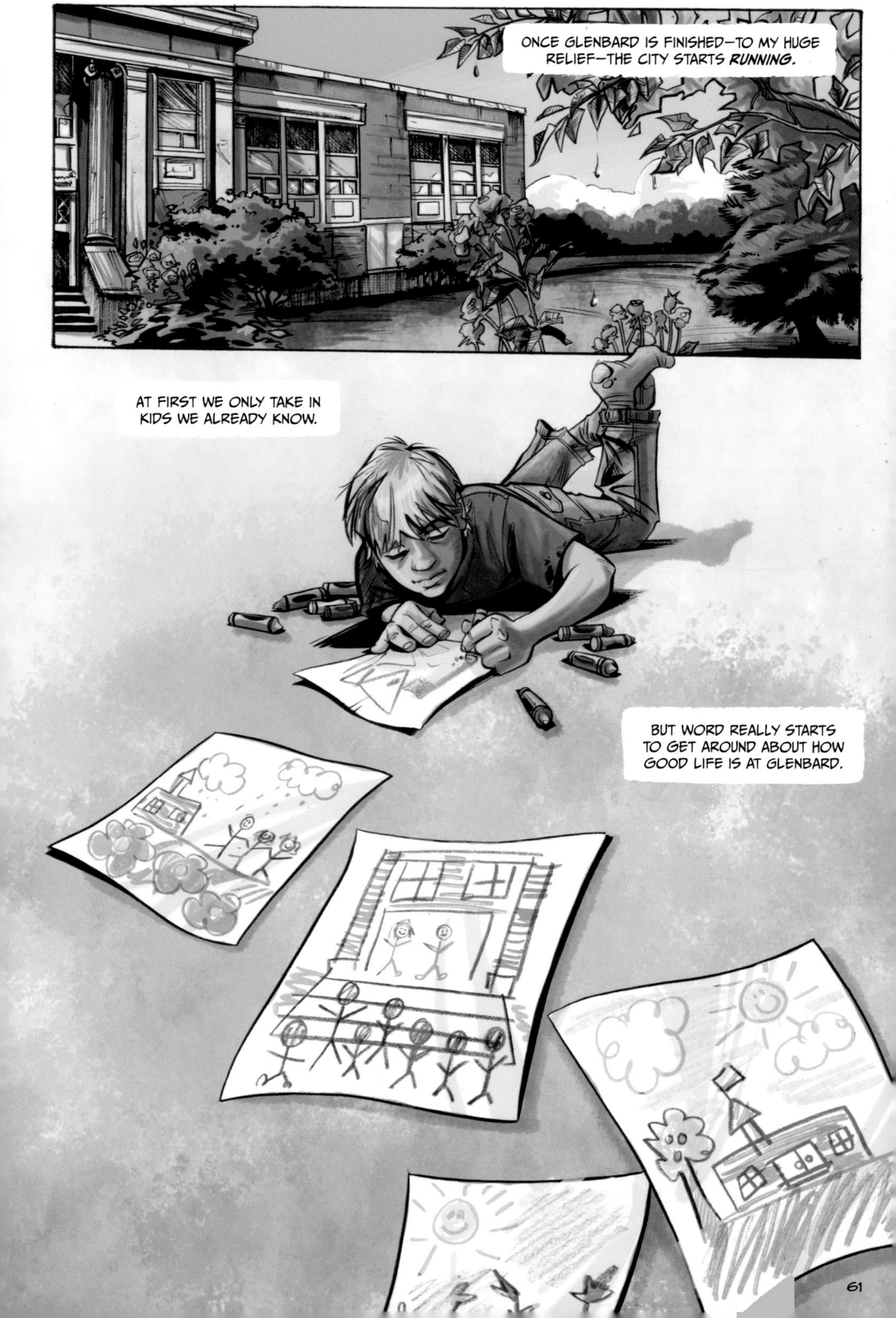
ONCE GLENBARD IS FINISHED—TO MY HUGE RELIEF—THE CITY STARTS *RUNNING.*
AT FIRST WE ONLY TAKE IN KIDS WE ALREADY KNOW.
BUT WORD REALLY STARTS TO GET AROUND ABOUT HOW GOOD LIFE IS AT GLENBARD.

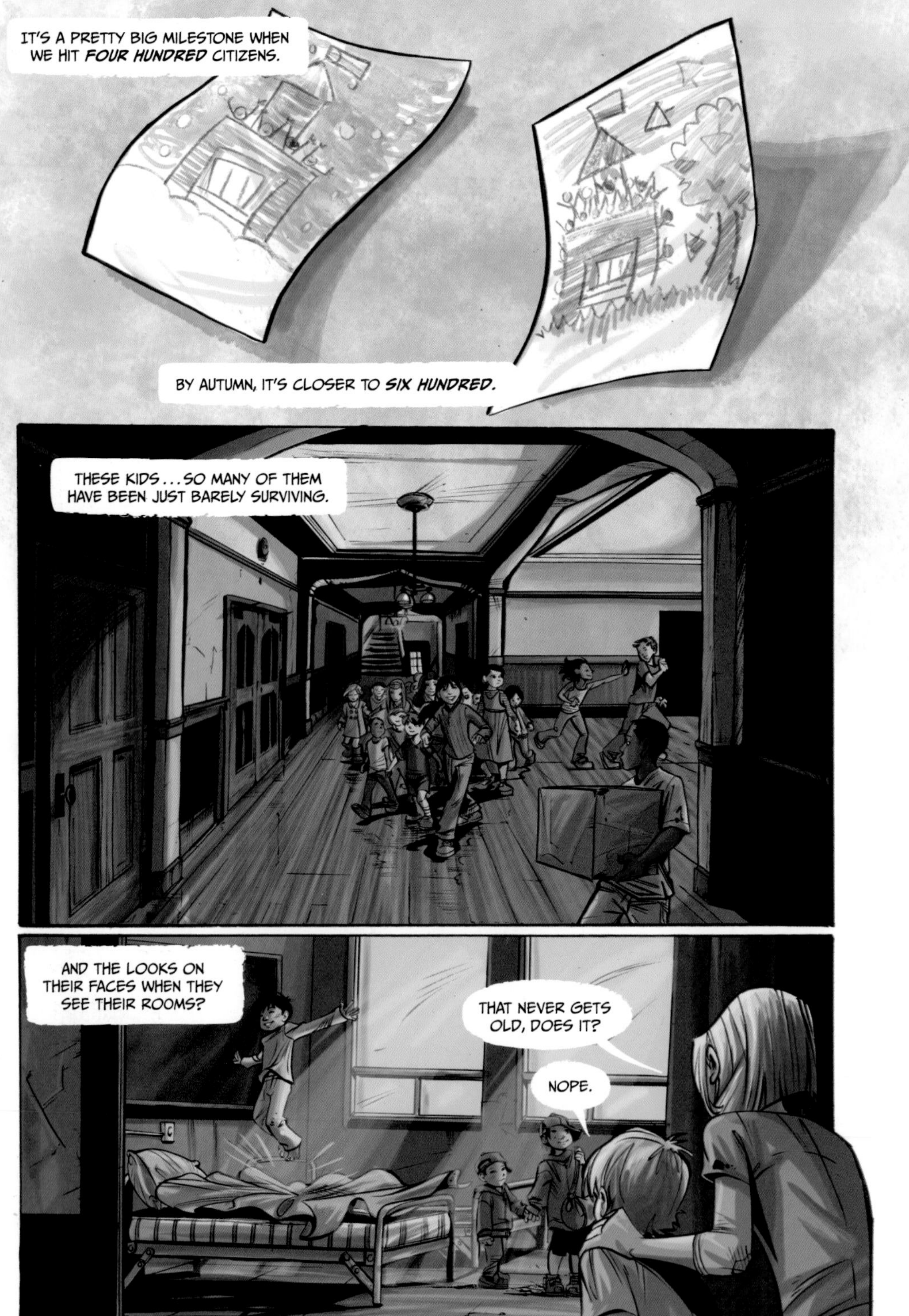
IT'S A PRETTY BIG MILESTONE WHEN WE HIT FOUR HUNDRED CITIZENS.
BY AUTUMN, IT'S CLOSER TO SIX HUNDRED.
THESE KIDS . . . SO MANY OF THEM HAVE BEEN JUST BARELY SURVIVING.
AND THE LOOKS ON THEIR FACES WHEN THEY SEE THEIR ROOMS?
THAT NEVER GETS OLD, DOES IT?
NOPE.

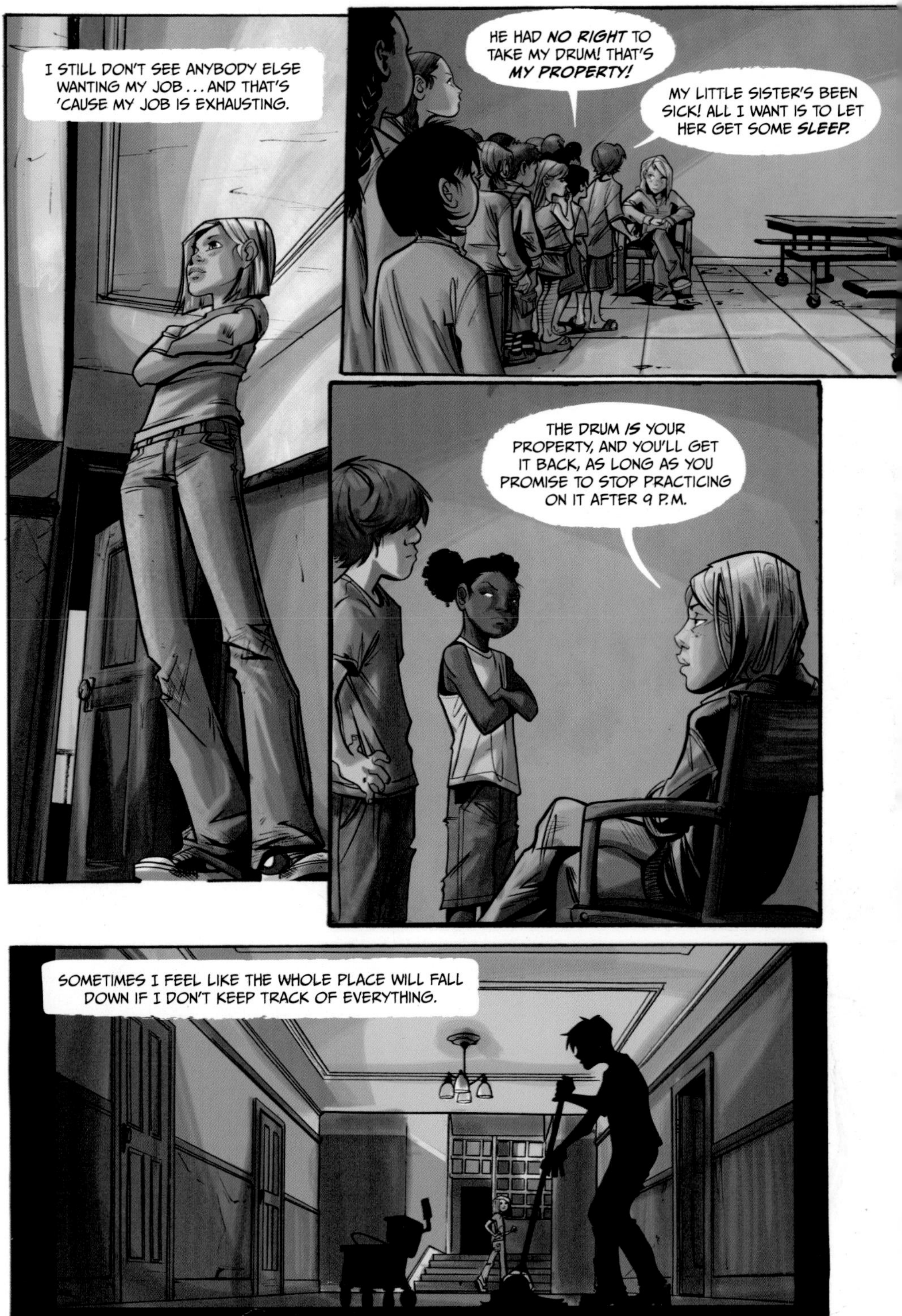
I STILL DON'T SEE ANYBODY ELSE WANTING MY JOB . . . AND THAT'S 'CAUSE MY JOB IS EXHAUSTING.
HE HAD *NO RIGHT* TO TAKE MY DRUM! THAT'S *MY PROPERTY!*
MY LITTLE SISTER'S BEEN SICK! ALL I WANT IS TO LET HER GET SOME *SLEEP.*
THE DRUM *IS* YOUR PROPERTY, AND YOU'LL GET IT BACK, AS LONG AS YOU PROMISE TO STOP PRACTICING ON IT AFTER 9 P.M.
SOMETIMES I FEEL LIKE THE WHOLE PLACE WILL FALL DOWN IF I DON'T KEEP TRACK OF EVERYTHING.

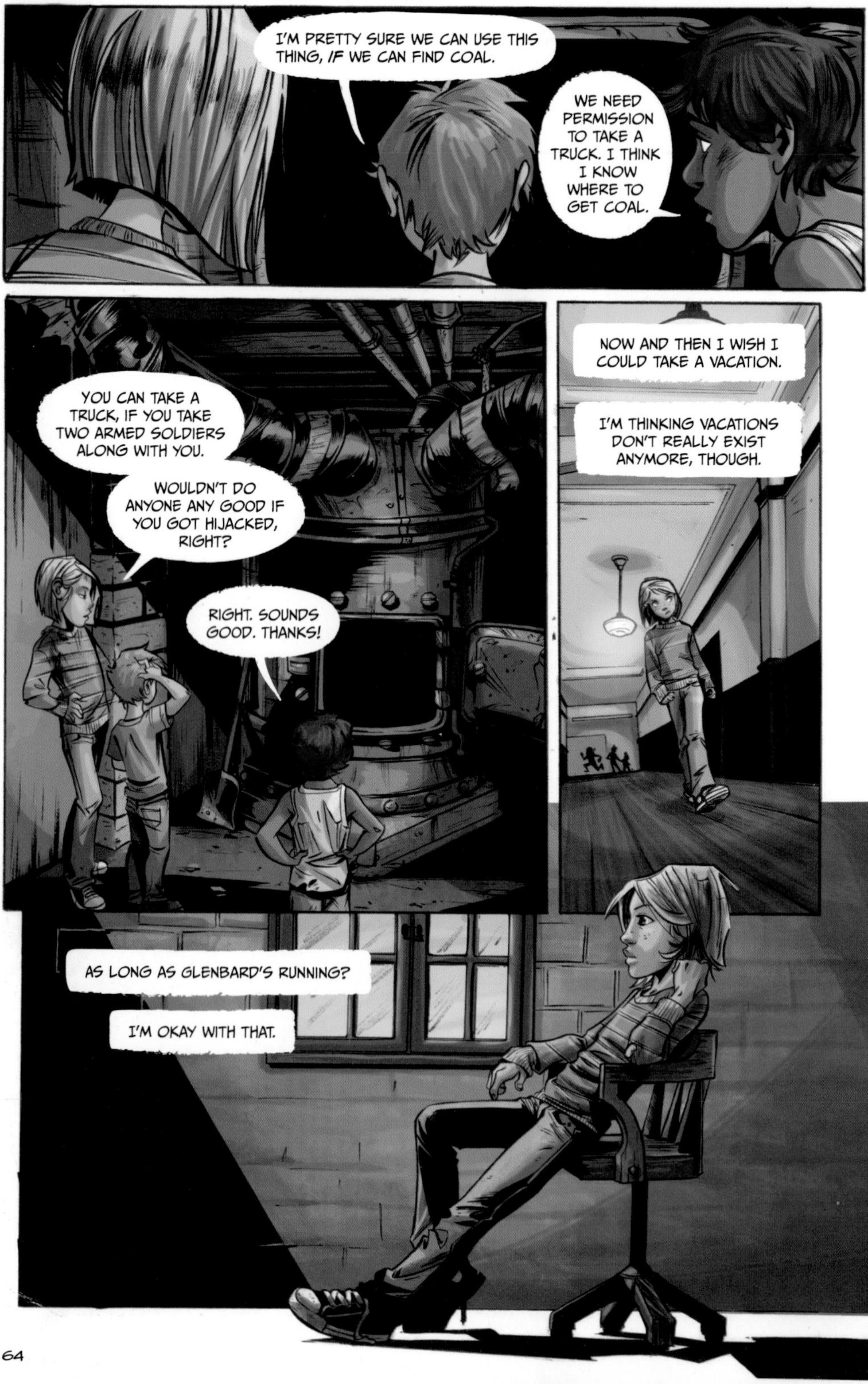
I'M PRETTY SURE WE CAN USE THIS THING, *IF* WE CAN FIND COAL.
WE NEED PERMISSION TO TAKE A TRUCK. I THINK I KNOW WHERE TO GET COAL.
YOU CAN TAKE A TRUCK, IF YOU TAKE TWO ARMED SOLDIERS ALONG WITH YOU.
WOULDN'T DO ANYONE ANY GOOD IF YOU GOT HIJACKED, RIGHT?
RIGHT. SOUNDS GOOD. THANKS!
NOW AND THEN I WISH I COULD TAKE A VACATION.
I'M THINKING VACATIONS DON'T REALLY EXIST ANYMORE, THOUGH.
AS LONG AS GLENBARD'S RUNNING?
I'M OKAY WITH THAT.

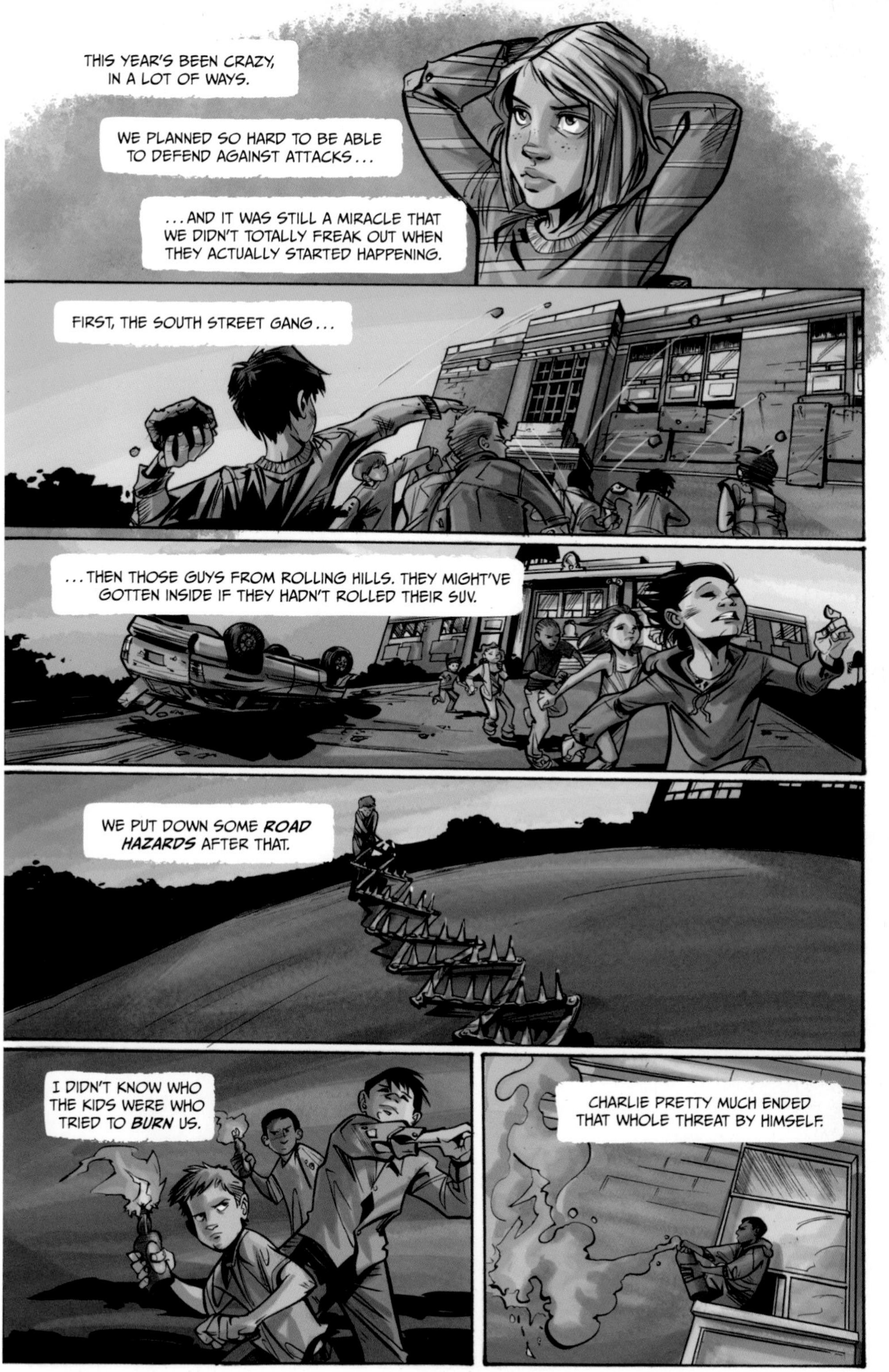

THIS YEAR'S BEEN CRAZY, IN A LOT OF WAYS.
WE PLANNED SO HARD TO BE ABLE TO DEFEND AGAINST ATTACKS...
...AND IT WAS STILL A MIRACLE THAT WE DIDN'T TOTALLY FREAK OUT WHEN THEY ACTUALLY STARTED HAPPENING.
FIRST, THE SOUTH STREET GANG...
...THEN THOSE GUYS FROM ROLLING HILLS. THEY MIGHT'VE GOTTEN INSIDE IF THEY HADN'T ROLLED THEIR SUV.
WE PUT DOWN SOME *ROAD HAZARDS* AFTER THAT.
I DIDN'T KNOW WHO THE KIDS WERE WHO TRIED TO *BURN* US.
CHARLIE PRETTY MUCH ENDED THAT WHOLE THREAT BY HIMSELF.

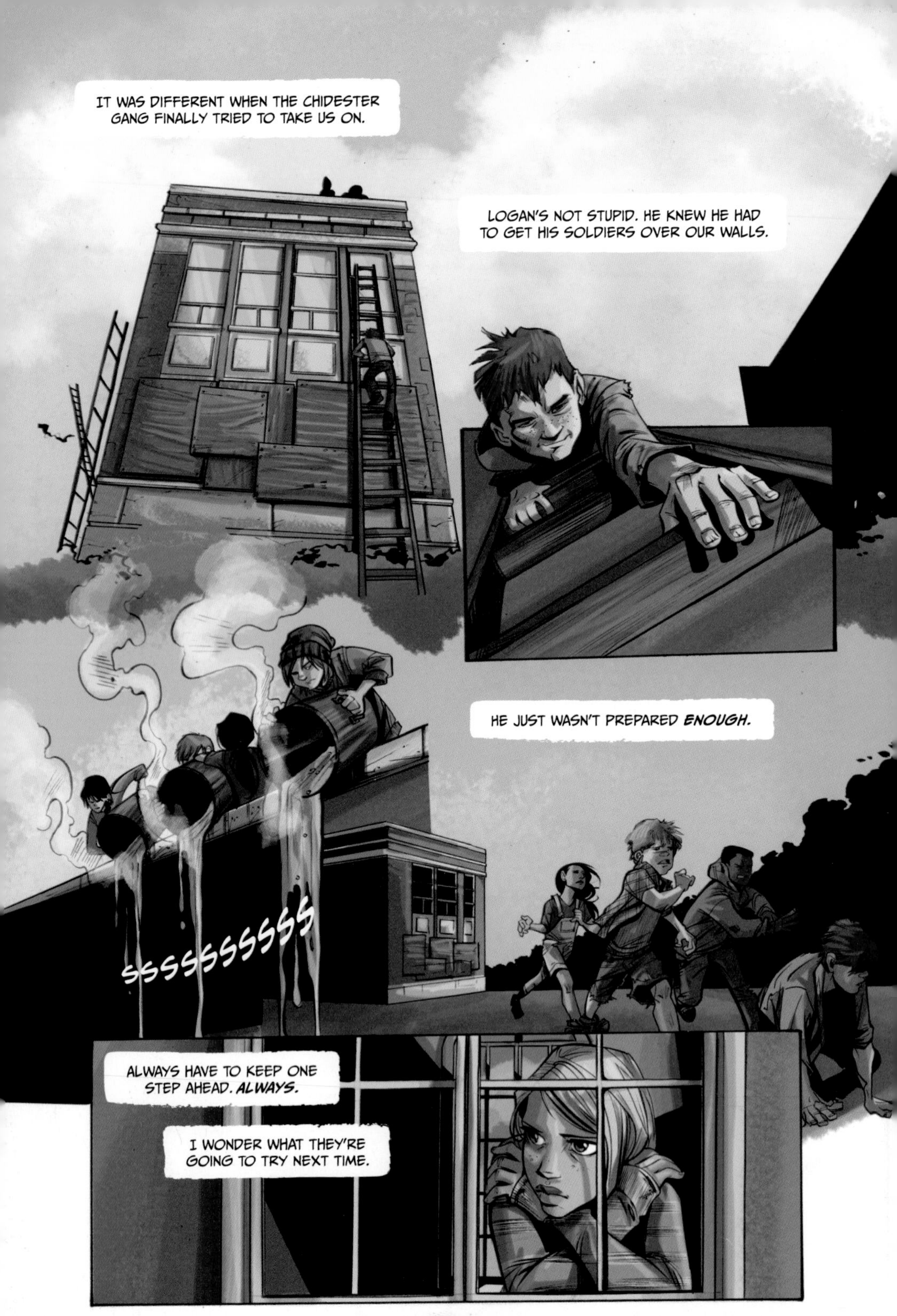
IT WAS DIFFERENT WHEN THE CHIDESTER GANG FINALLY TRIED TO TAKE US ON.
LOGAN'S NOT STUPID. HE KNEW HE HAD TO GET HIS SOLDIERS OVER OUR WALLS.
HE JUST WASN'T PREPARED ENOUGH.
SSSSSSSSSSS
ALWAYS HAVE TO KEEP ONE STEP AHEAD. ALWAYS.
I WONDER WHAT THEY'RE GOING TO TRY NEXT TIME.

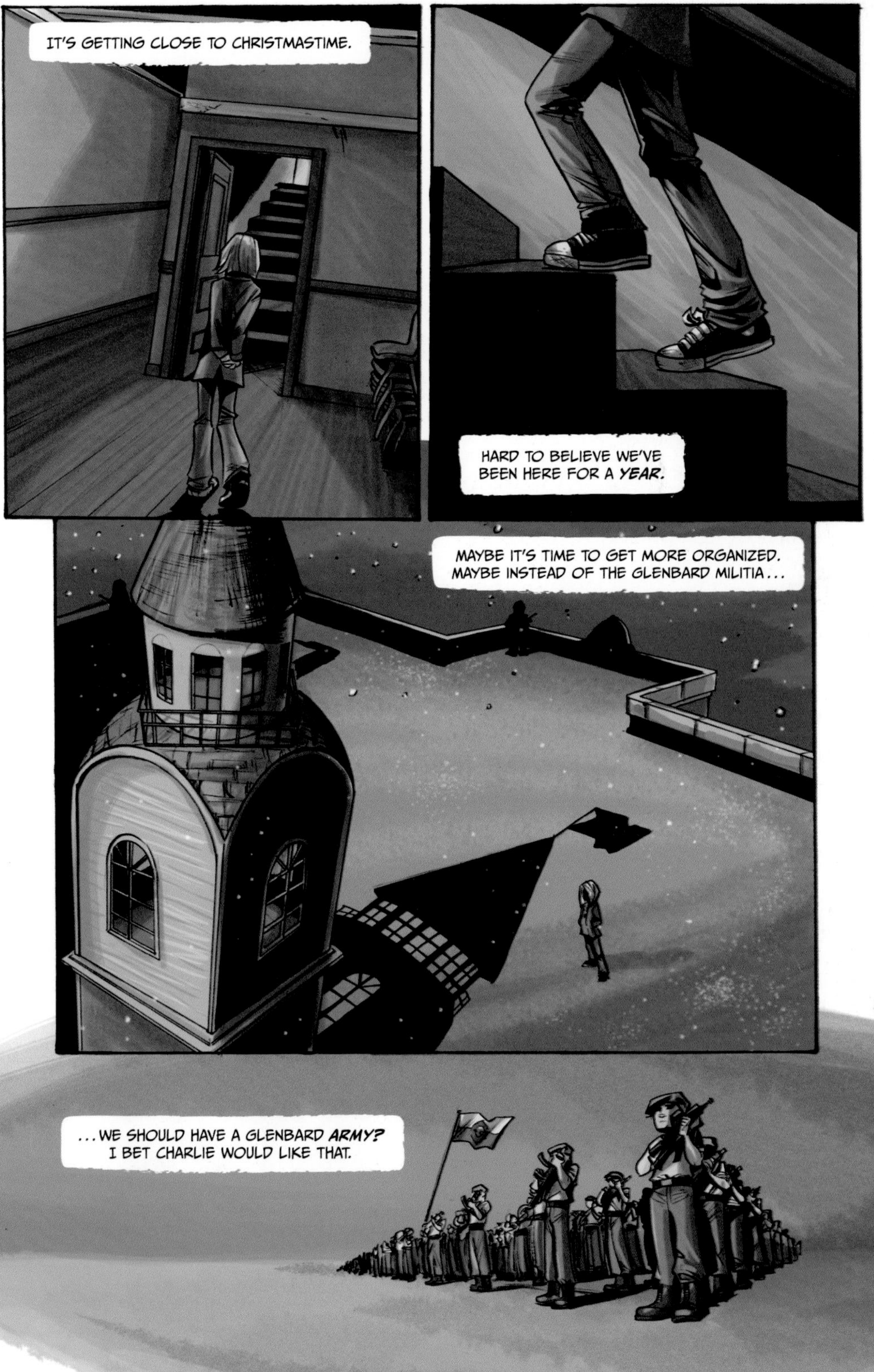
IT'S GETTING CLOSE TO CHRISTMASTIME.
HARD TO BELIEVE WE'VE BEEN HERE FOR A *YEAR.*
MAYBE IT'S TIME TO GET MORE ORGANIZED. MAYBE INSTEAD OF THE GLENBARD MILITIA...
...WE SHOULD HAVE A GLENBARD *ARMY?* I BET CHARLIE WOULD LIKE THAT.

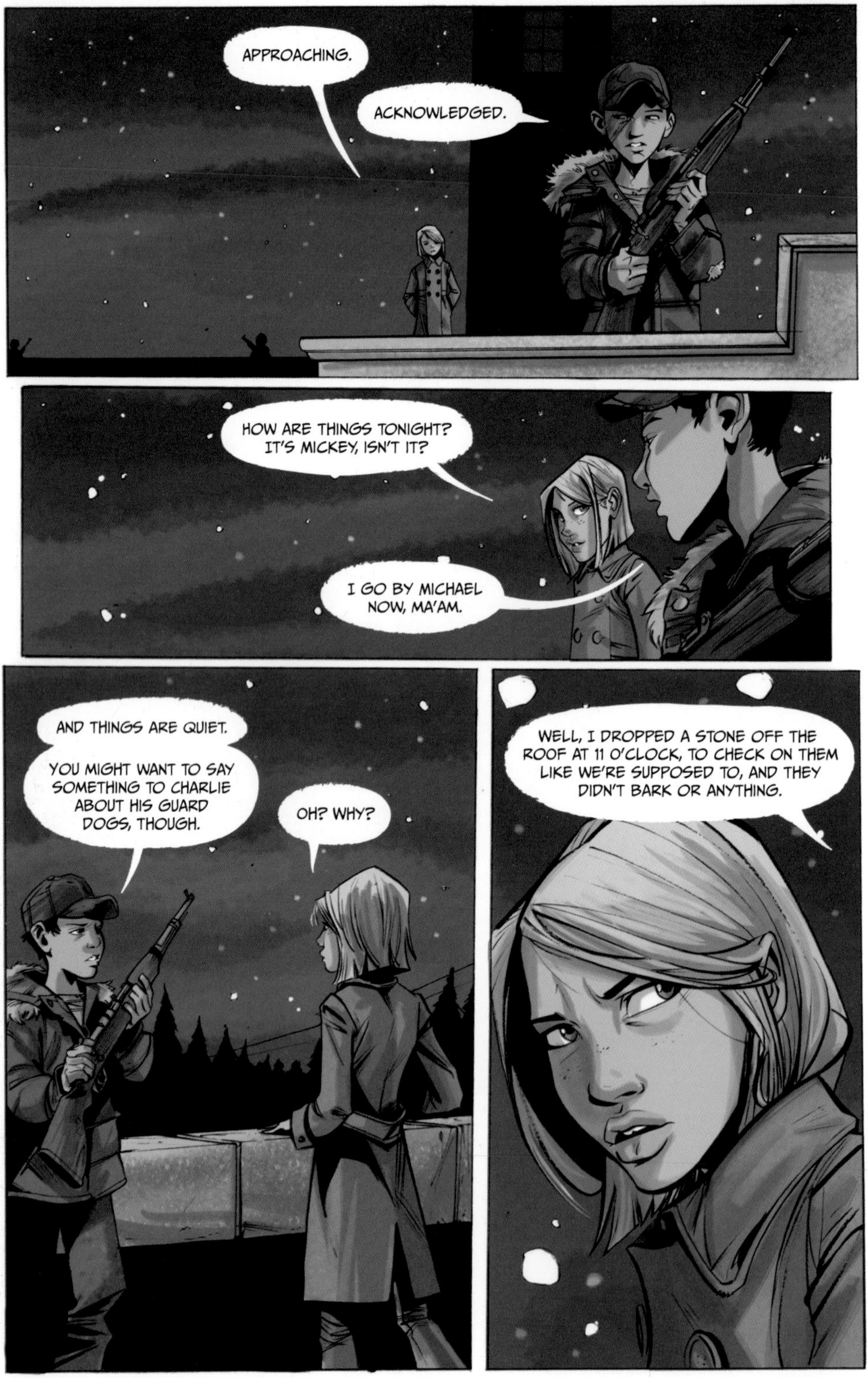
APPROACHING.
ACKNOWLEDGED.
HOW ARE THINGS TONIGHT? IT'S MICKEY, ISN'T IT?
I GO BY MICHAEL NOW, MA'AM.
AND THINGS ARE QUIET.
YOU MIGHT WANT TO SAY SOMETHING TO CHARLIE ABOUT HIS GUARD DOGS, THOUGH.
OH? WHY?
WELL, I DROPPED A STONE OFF THE ROOF AT 11 O'CLOCK, TO CHECK ON THEM LIKE WE'RE SUPPOSED TO, AND THEY DIDN'T BARK OR ANYTHING.

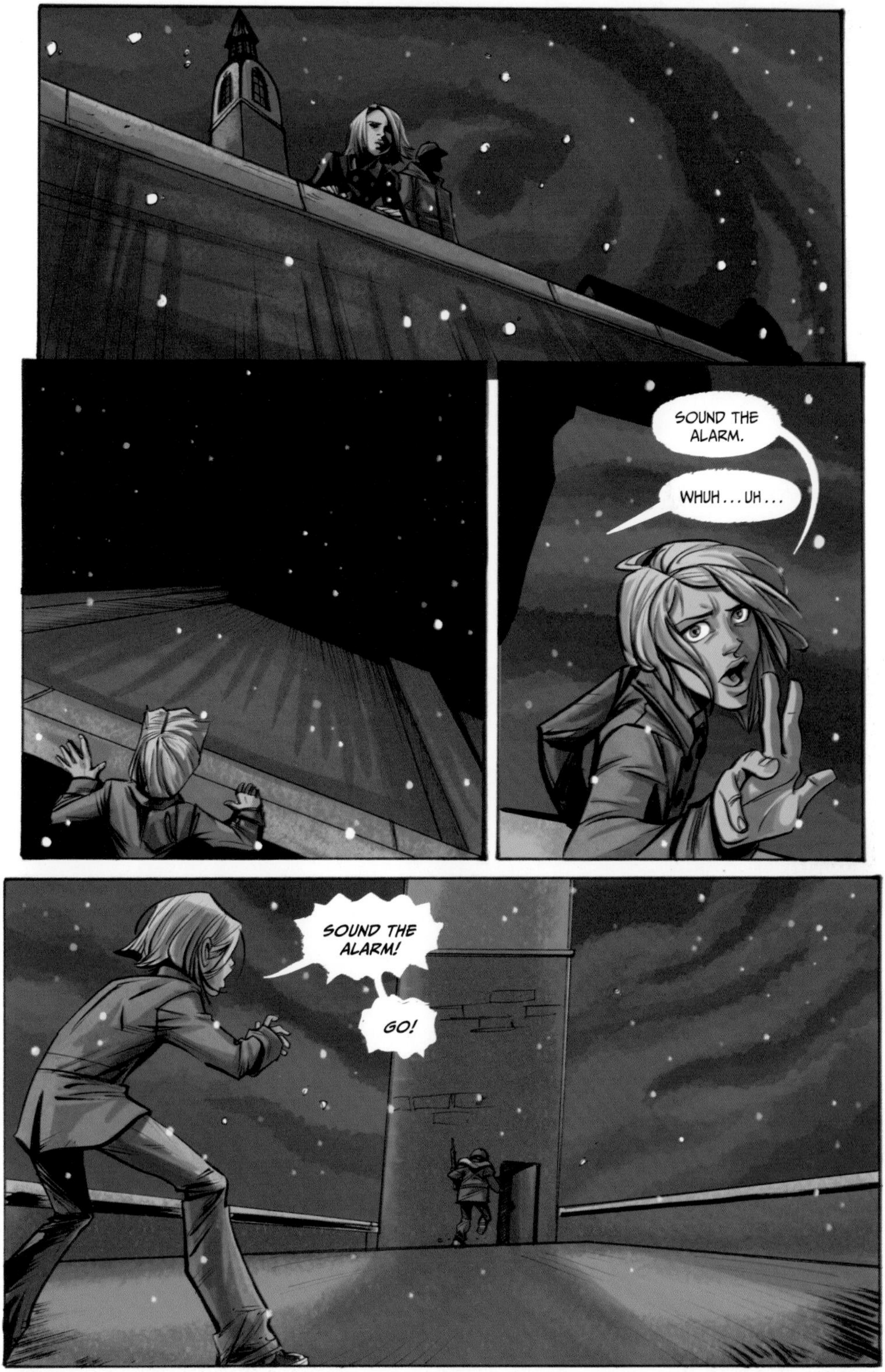
SOUND THE ALARM.
WHUH . . . UH . . .
SOUND THE ALARM!
GO!

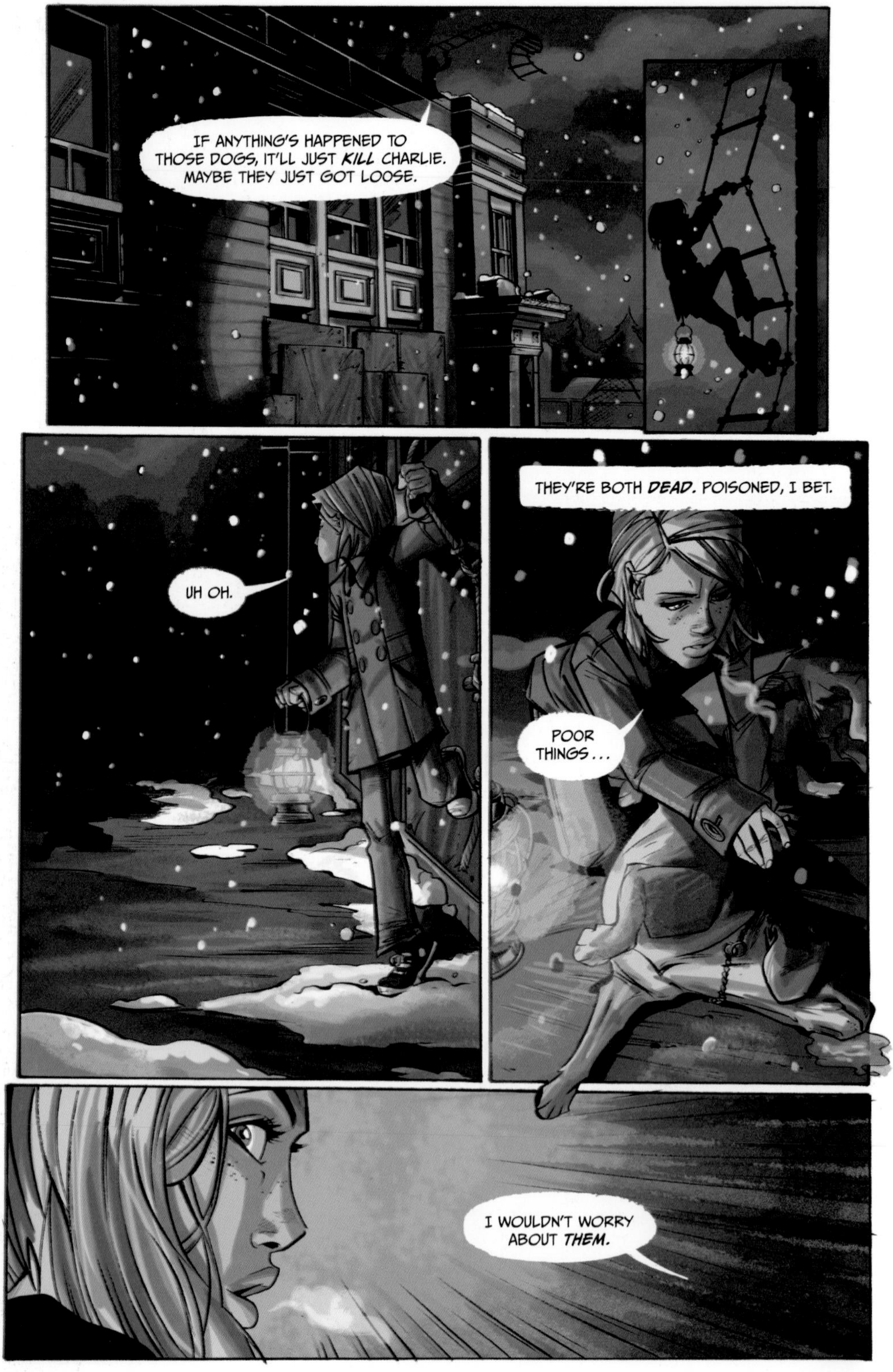
IF ANYTHING'S HAPPENED TO THOSE DOGS, IT'LL JUST KILL CHARLIE. MAYBE THEY JUST GOT LOOSE.
UH OH.
THEY'RE BOTH DEAD. POISONED, I BET.
POOR THINGS...
I WOULDN'T WORRY ABOUT THEM.

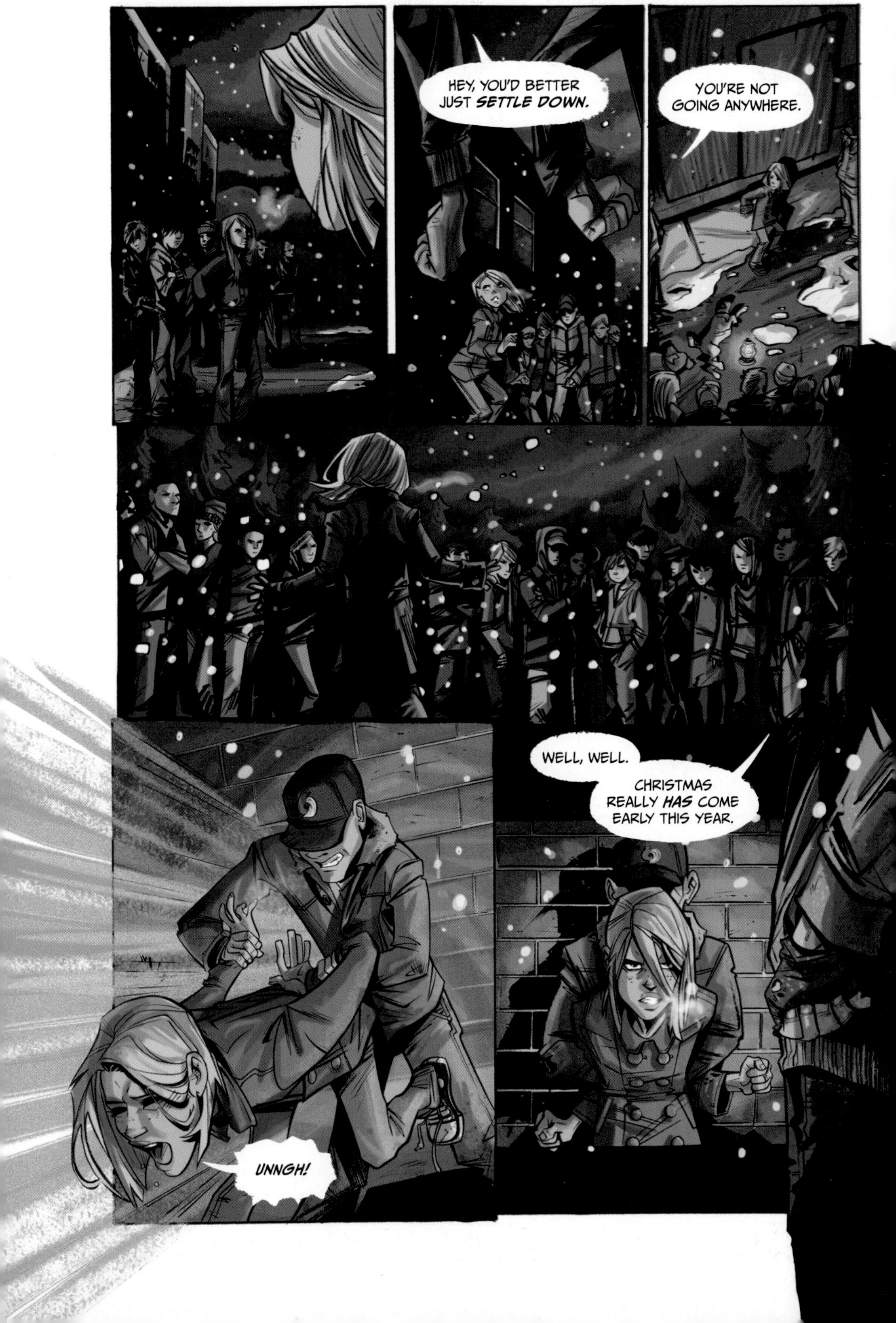
HEY, YOU'D BETTER JUST SETTLE DOWN.
YOU'RE NOT GOING ANYWHERE.
UNNGH!
WELL, WELL.
CHRISTMAS REALLY HAS COME EARLY THIS YEAR.

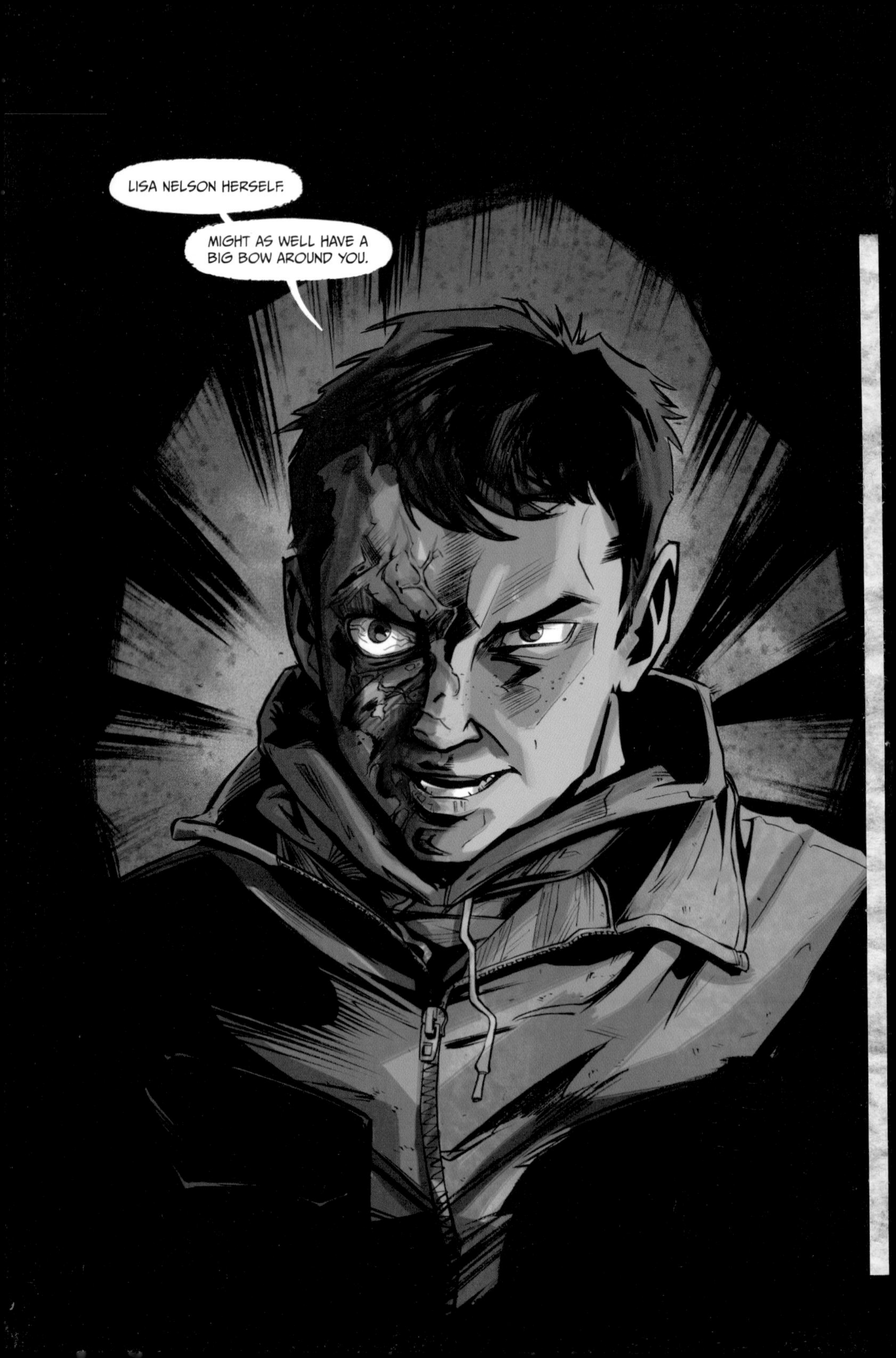
LISA NELSON HERSELF.
MIGHT AS WELL HAVE A BIG BOW AROUND YOU.

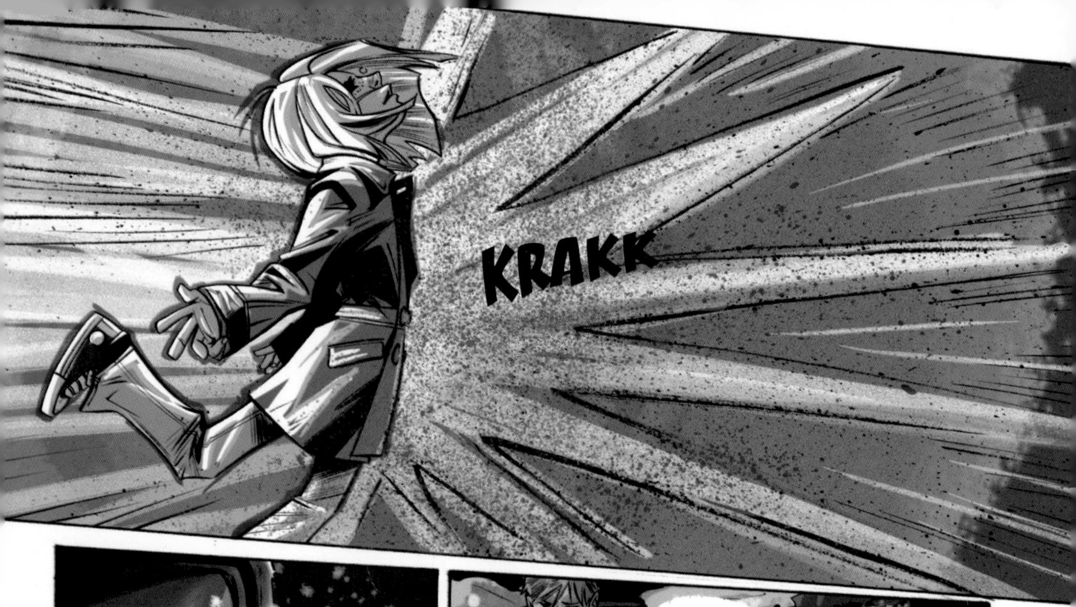
KRAKK

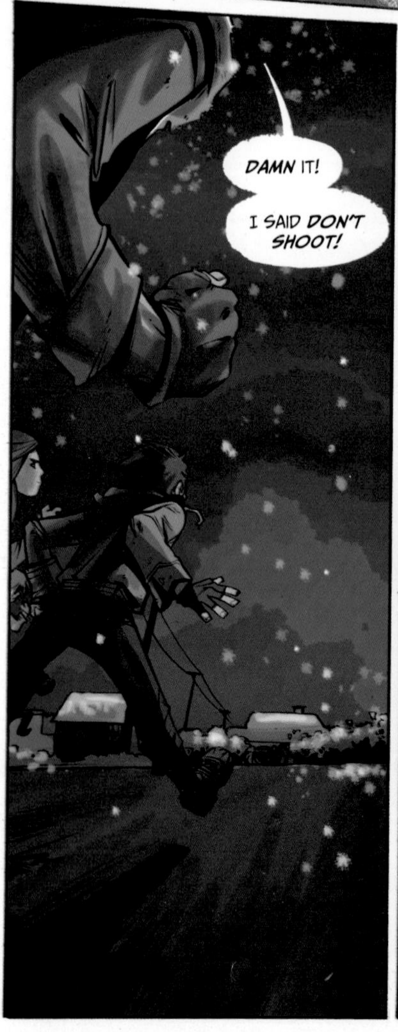
DAMN IT!
I SAID DON'T SHOOT!

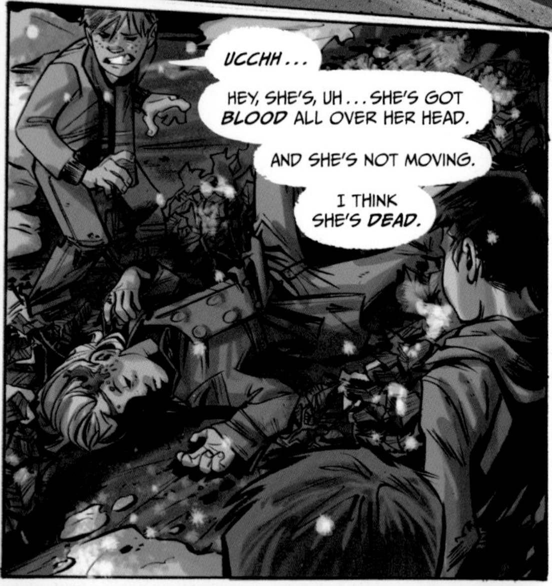
UCCHH . . .
HEY, SHE'S, UH . . . SHE'S GOT BLOOD ALL OVER HER HEAD.
AND SHE'S NOT MOVING.
I THINK SHE'S DEAD.

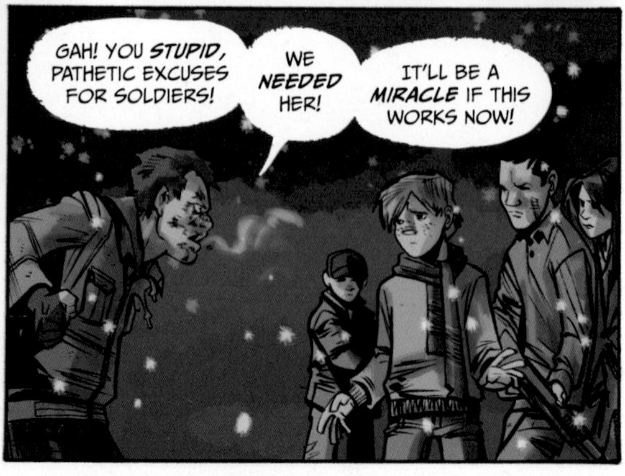
GAH! YOU STUPID, PATHETIC EXCUSES FOR SOLDIERS!
WE NEEDED HER!
IT'LL BE A MIRACLE IF THIS WORKS NOW!

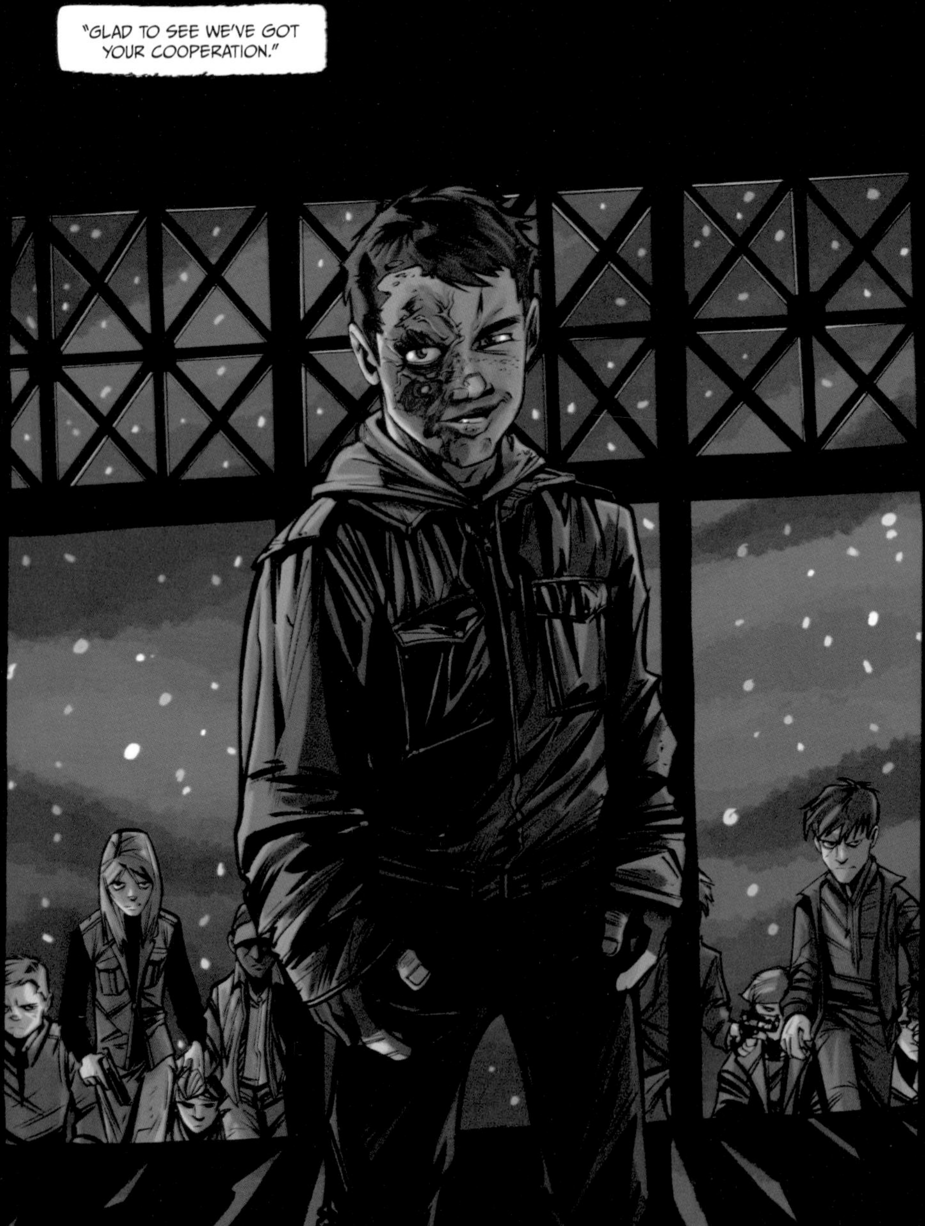
"GLAD TO SEE WE'VE GOT YOUR COOPERATION."

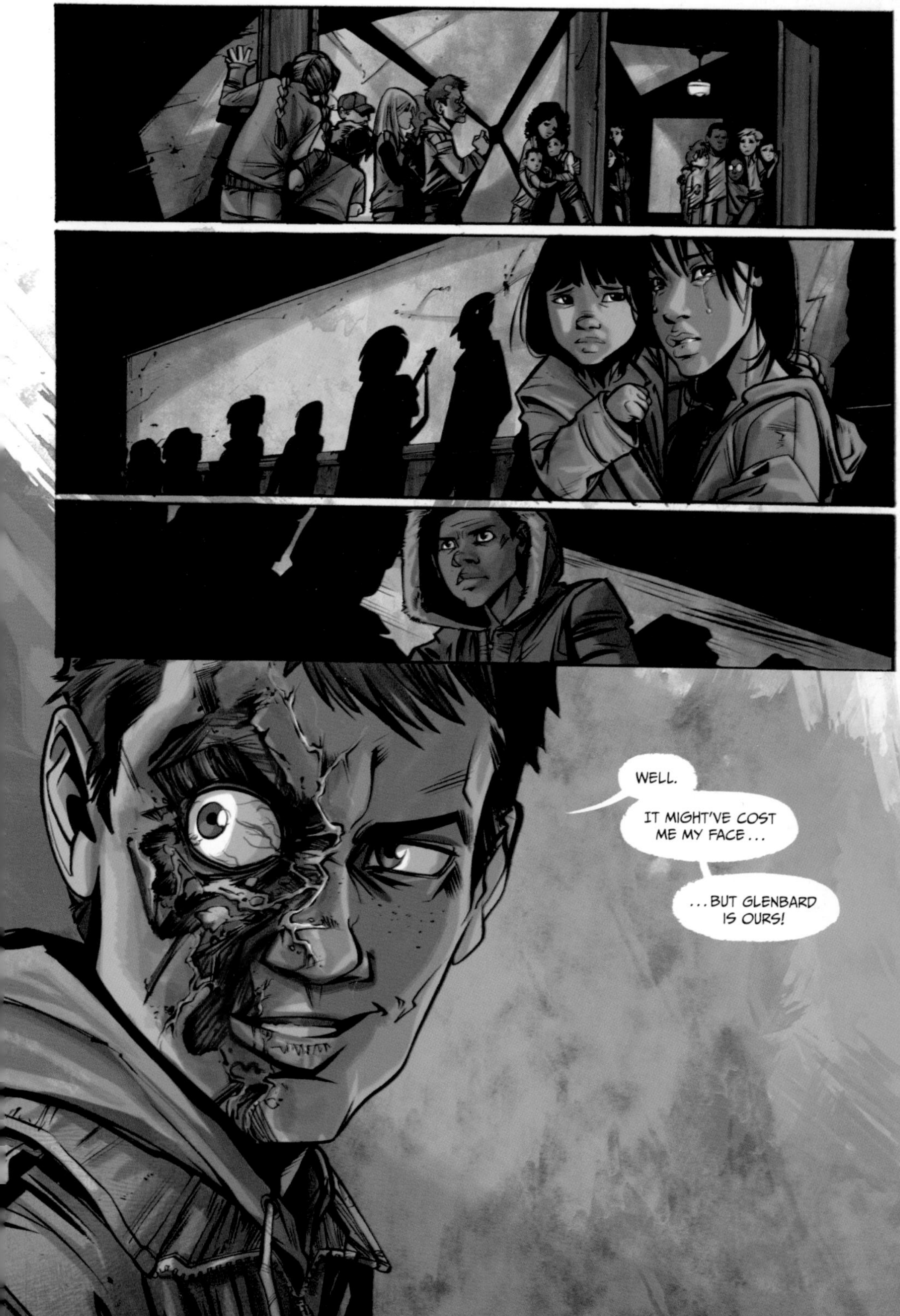
WELL.
IT MIGHT'VE COST ME MY FACE...
...BUT GLENBARD IS OURS!

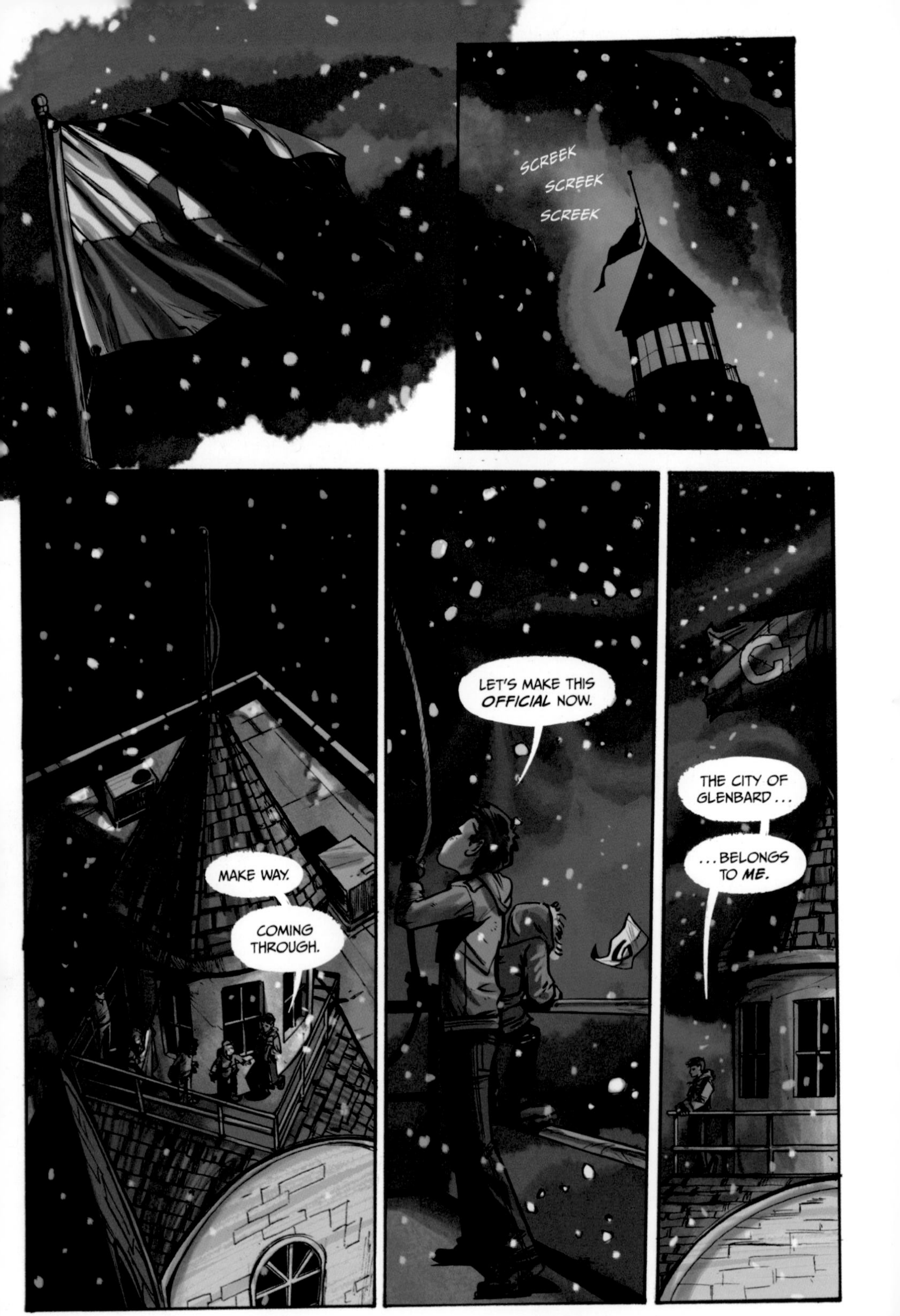
SCREEK
SCREEK
SCREEK
MAKE WAY.
COMING THROUGH.
LET'S MAKE THIS OFFICIAL NOW.
THE CITY OF GLENBARD . . .
. . . BELONGS TO ME.

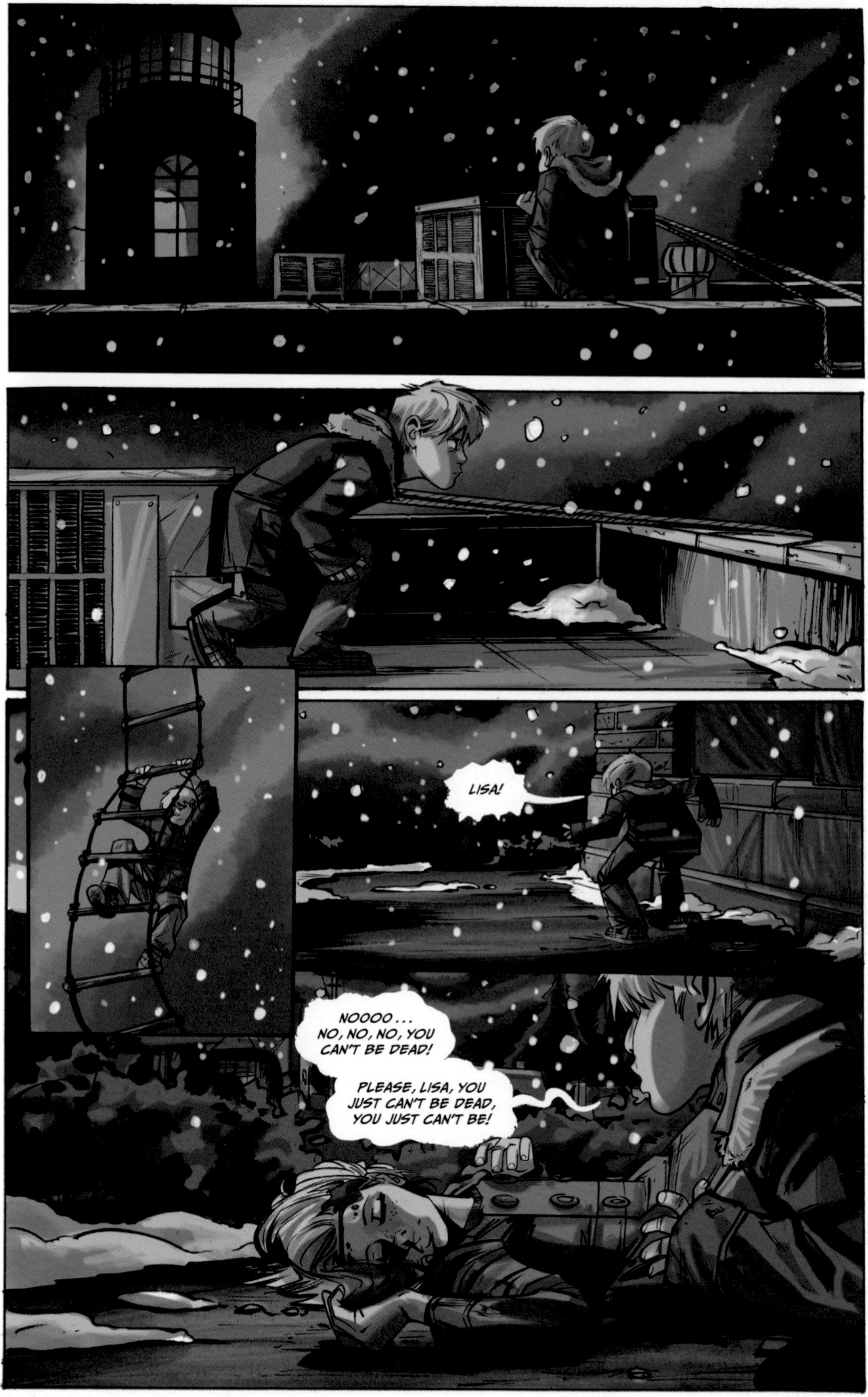
LISA!
NOOOO . . .
NO, NO, NO, YOU
CAN'T BE DEAD!
PLEASE, LISA, YOU
JUST CAN'T BE DEAD,
YOU JUST CAN'T BE!

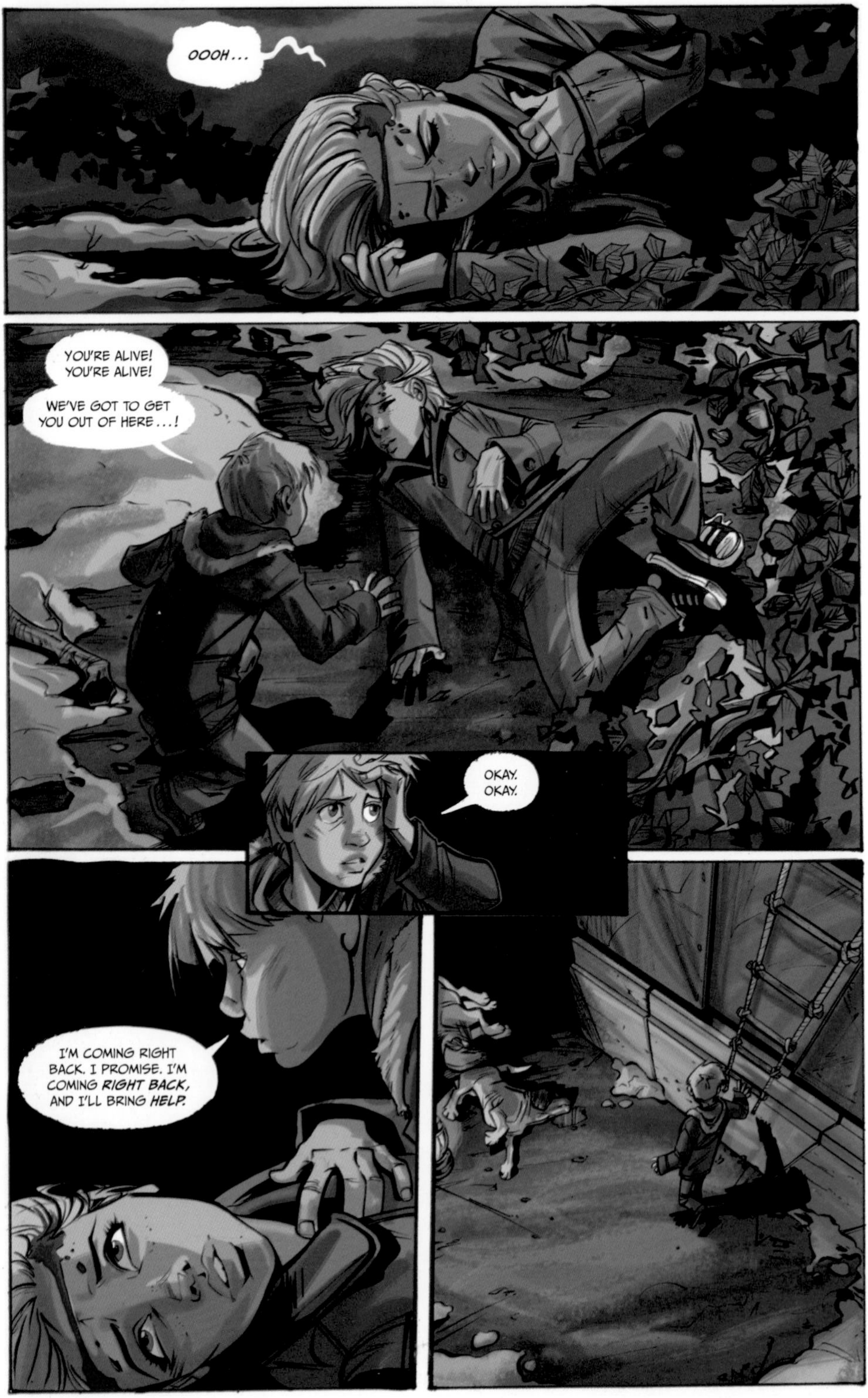
OOOH...
YOU'RE ALIVE! YOU'RE ALIVE!
WE'VE GOT TO GET YOU OUT OF HERE...!
OKAY. OKAY.
I'M COMING RIGHT BACK. I PROMISE. I'M COMING RIGHT BACK, AND I'LL BRING HELP.

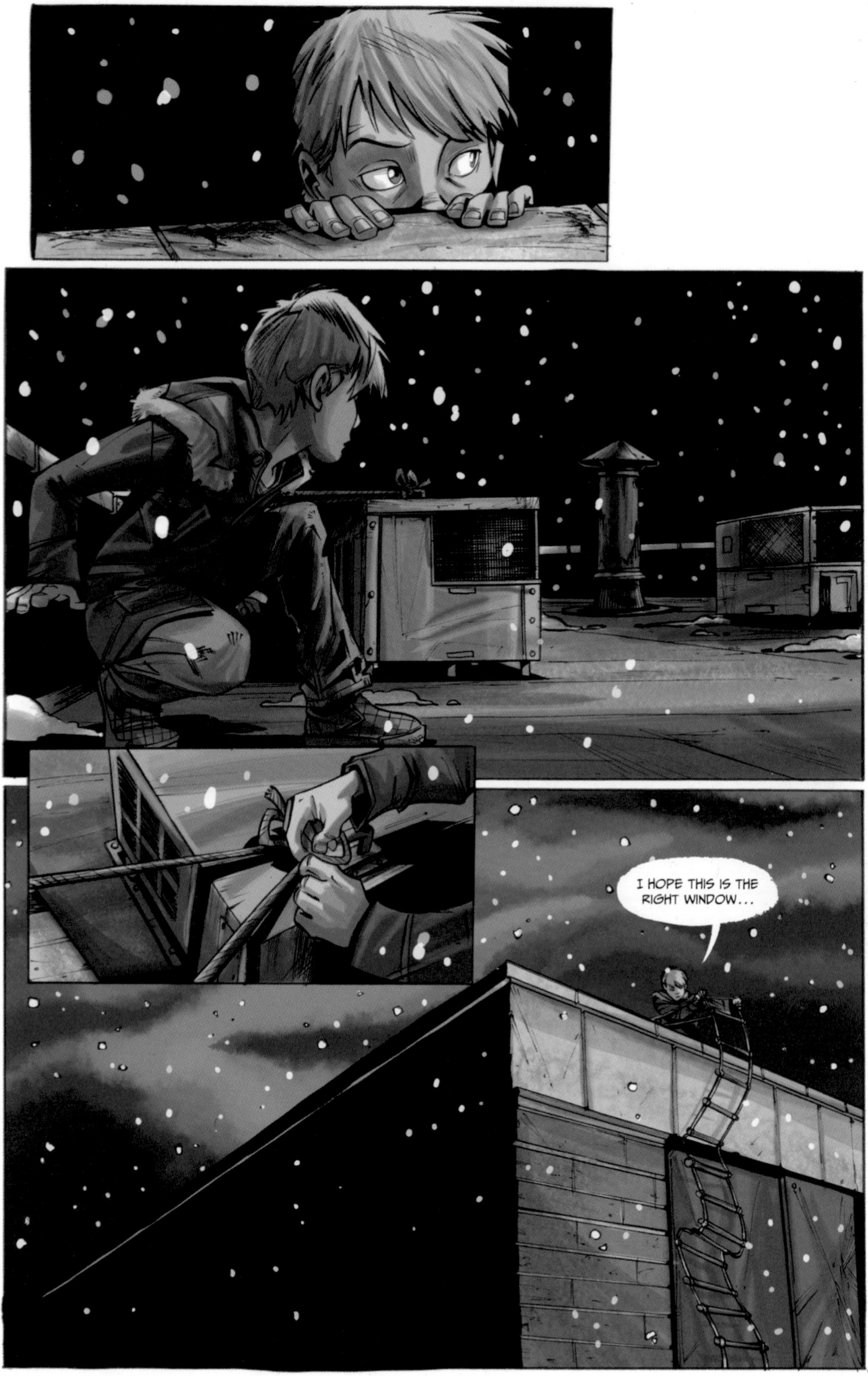
I HOPE THIS IS THE RIGHT WINDOW...

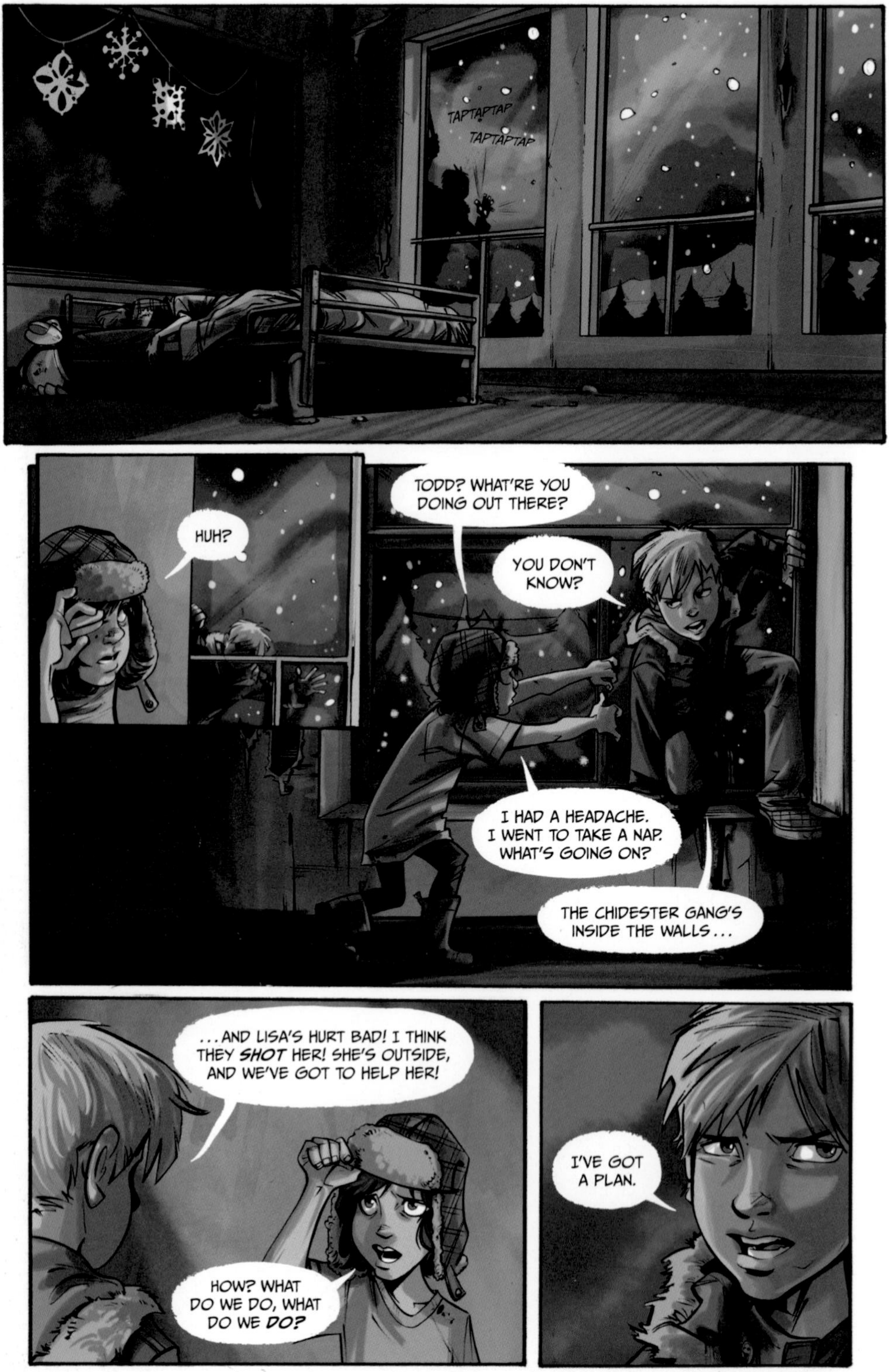
TAPTAPTAP
TAPTAPTAP
HUH?
TODD? WHAT'RE YOU DOING OUT THERE?
YOU DON'T KNOW?
I HAD A HEADACHE. I WENT TO TAKE A NAP. WHAT'S GOING ON?
THE CHIDESTER GANG'S INSIDE THE WALLS...
...AND LISA'S HURT BAD! I THINK THEY *SHOT* HER! SHE'S OUTSIDE, AND WE'VE GOT TO HELP HER!
HOW? WHAT DO WE DO, WHAT DO WE *DO?*
I'VE GOT A PLAN.

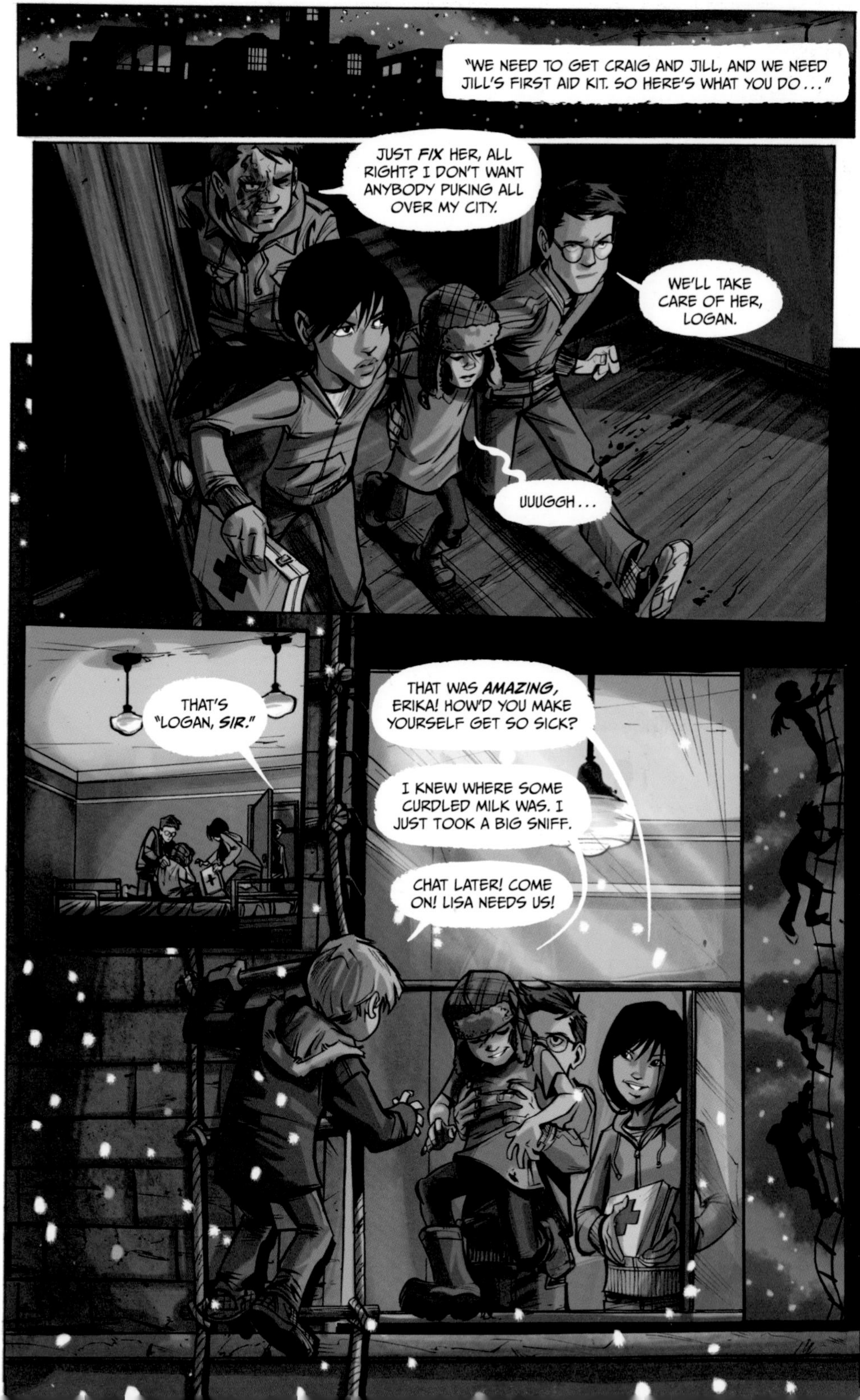
"WE NEED TO GET CRAIG AND JILL, AND WE NEED JILL'S FIRST AID KIT. SO HERE'S WHAT YOU DO . . ."
JUST FIX HER, ALL RIGHT? I DON'T WANT ANYBODY PUKING ALL OVER MY CITY.
WE'LL TAKE CARE OF HER, LOGAN.
UUUGGH . . .
THAT'S "LOGAN, SIR."
THAT WAS AMAZING, ERIKA! HOW'D YOU MAKE YOURSELF GET SO SICK?
I KNEW WHERE SOME CURDLED MILK WAS. I JUST TOOK A BIG SNIFF.
CHAT LATER! COME ON! LISA NEEDS US!

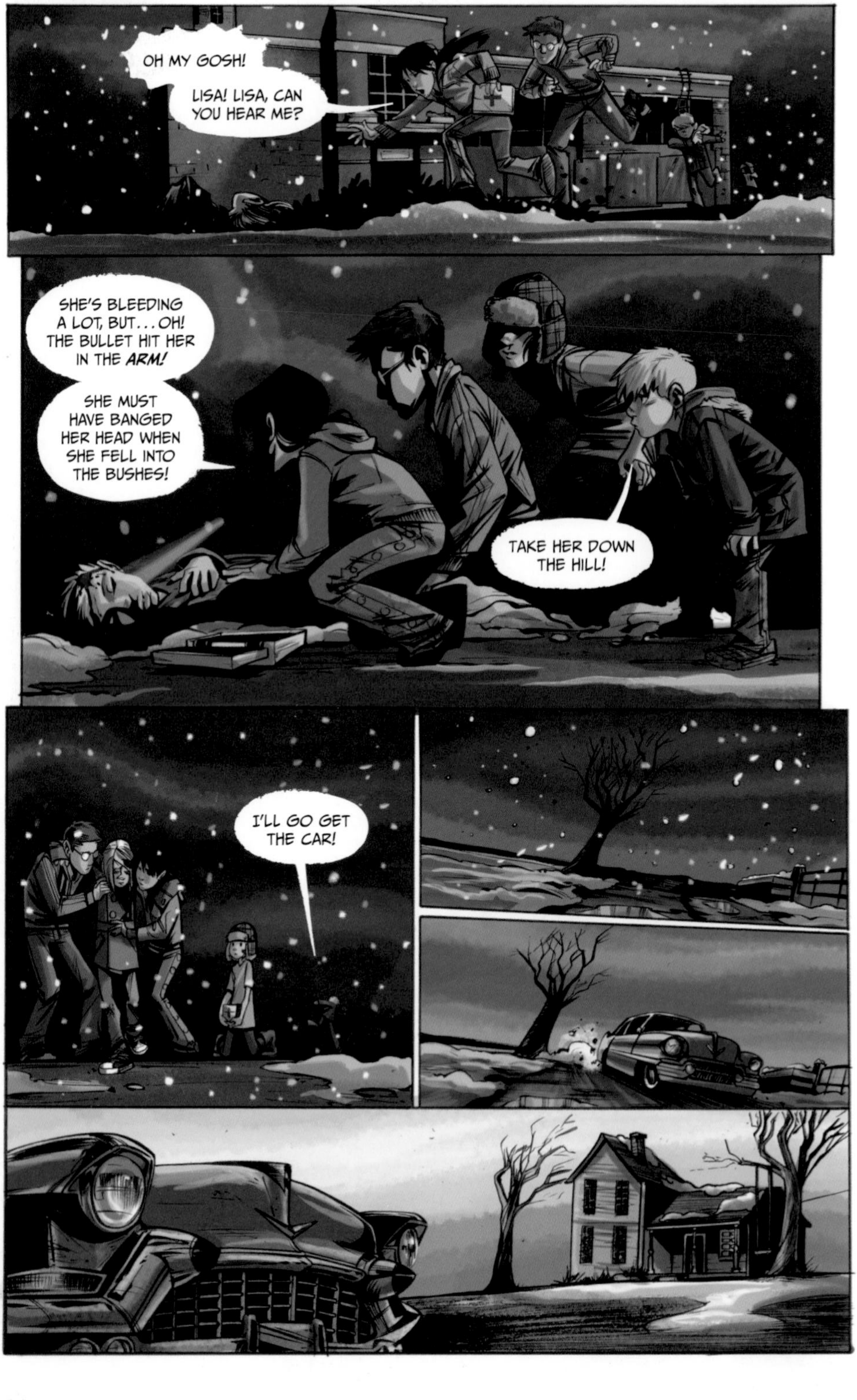
OH MY GOSH!
LISA! LISA, CAN YOU HEAR ME?
SHE'S BLEEDING A LOT, BUT...OH! THE BULLET HIT HER IN THE *ARM!*
SHE MUST HAVE BANGED HER HEAD WHEN SHE FELL INTO THE BUSHES!
TAKE HER DOWN THE HILL!
I'LL GO GET THE CAR!

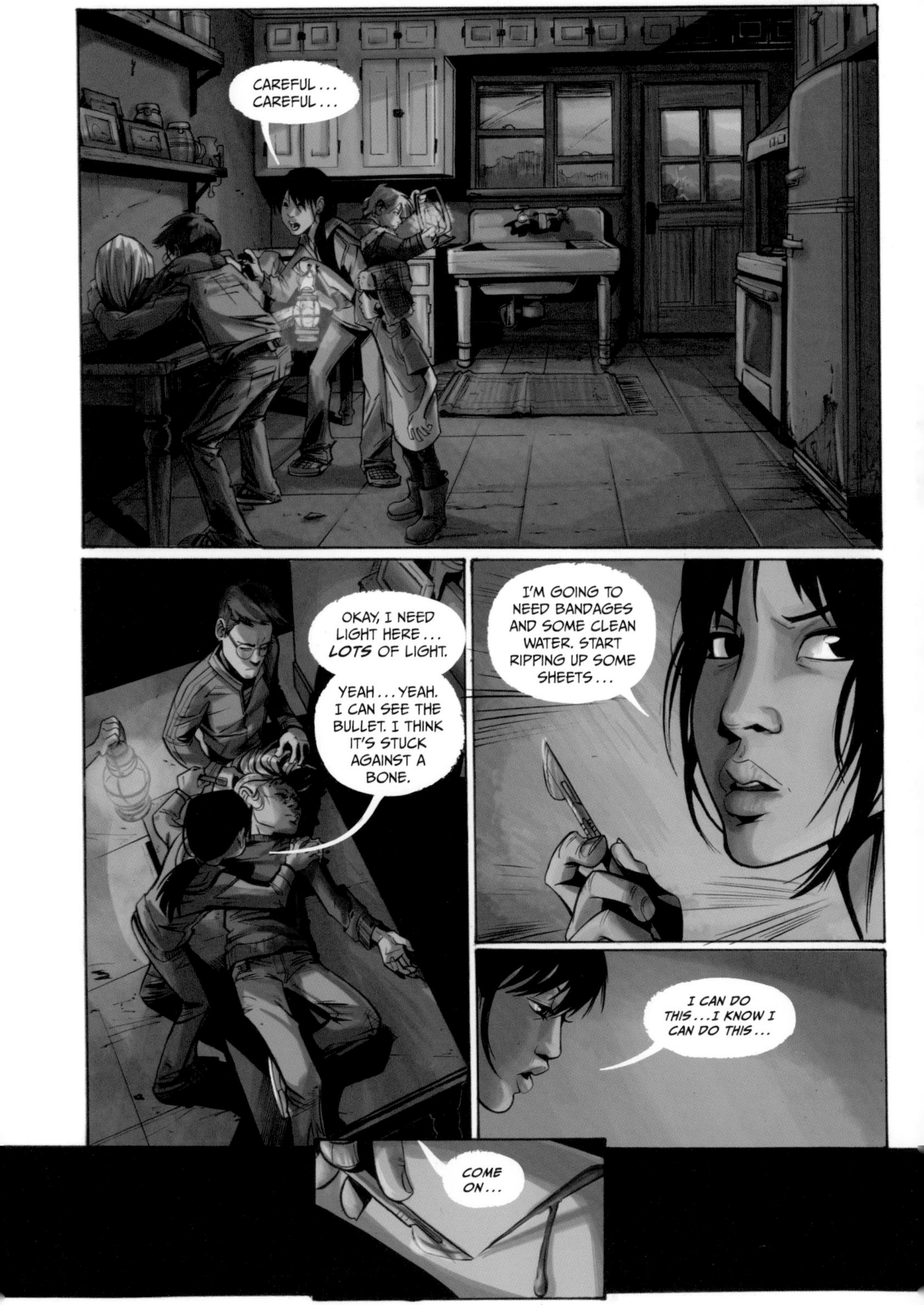
CAREFUL . . .
CAREFUL . . .
OKAY, I NEED LIGHT HERE . . . LOTS OF LIGHT.
YEAH . . . YEAH. I CAN SEE THE BULLET. I THINK IT'S STUCK AGAINST A BONE.
I'M GOING TO NEED BANDAGES AND SOME CLEAN WATER. START RIPPING UP SOME SHEETS . . .
I CAN DO THIS . . . I KNOW I CAN DO THIS . . .
COME ON . . .

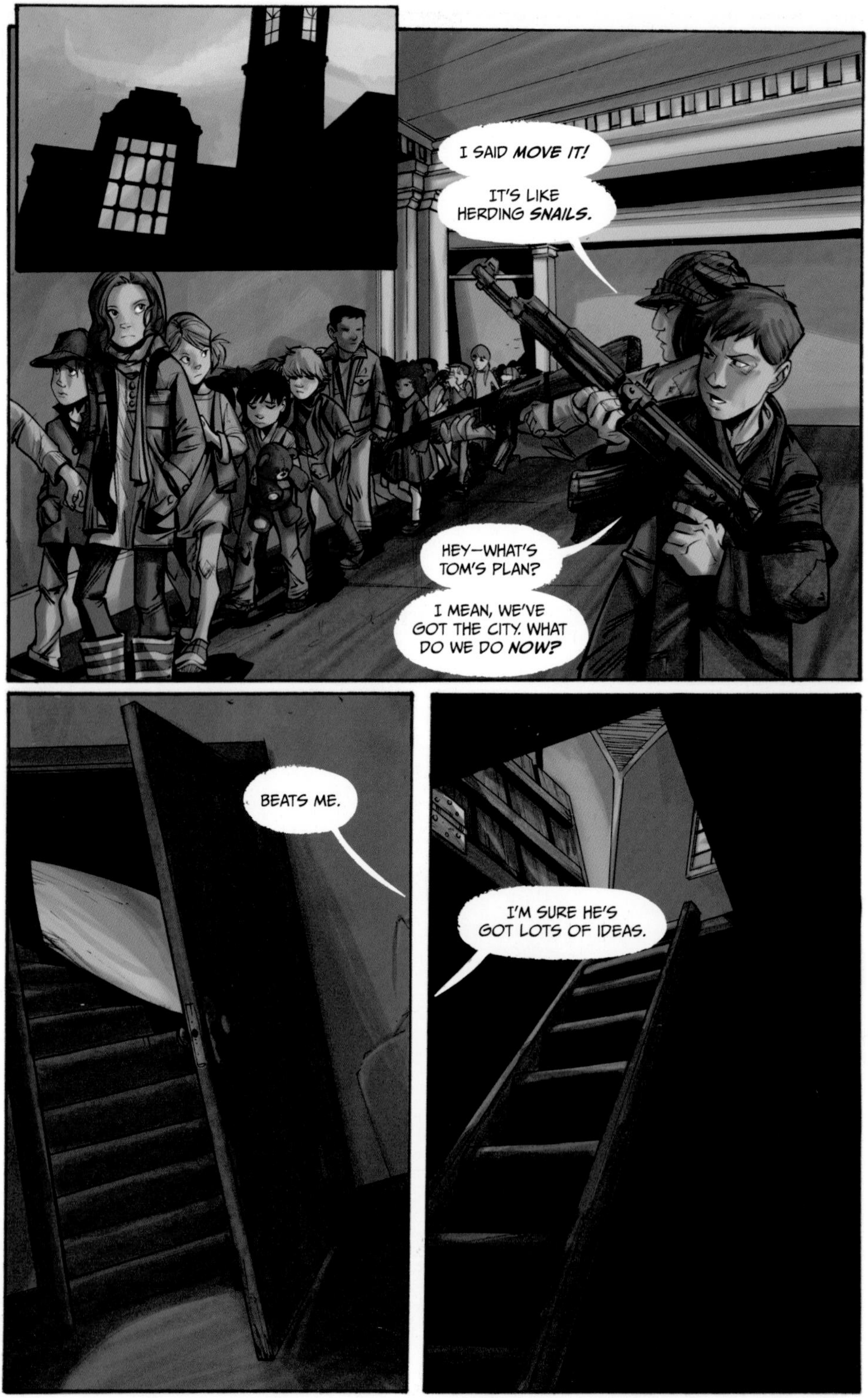
I SAID MOVE IT!
IT'S LIKE HERDING SNAILS.
HEY—WHAT'S TOM'S PLAN?
I MEAN, WE'VE GOT THE CITY. WHAT DO WE DO NOW?
BEATS ME.
I'M SURE HE'S GOT LOTS OF IDEAS.

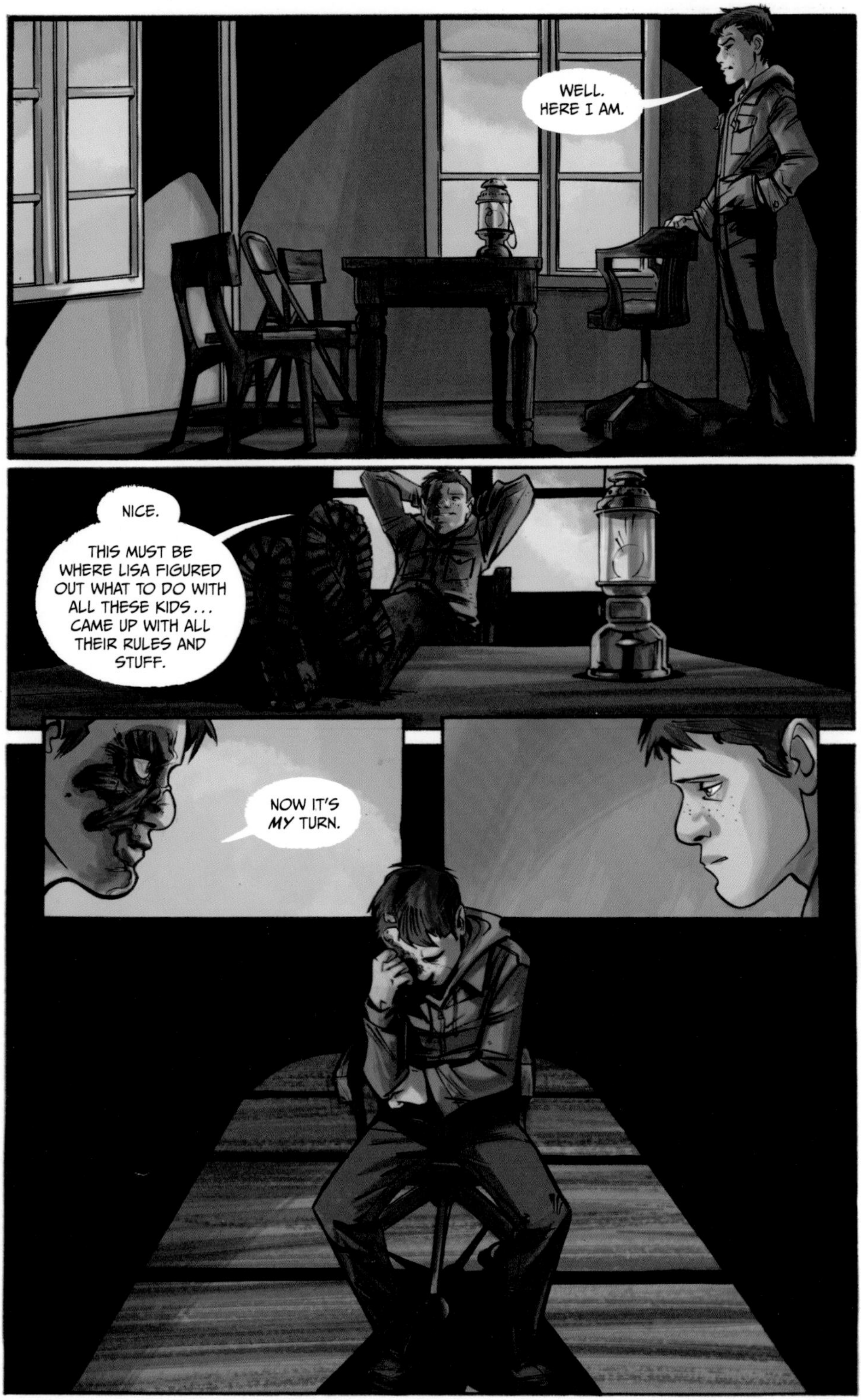
WELL. HERE I AM.
NICE.
THIS MUST BE WHERE LISA FIGURED OUT WHAT TO DO WITH ALL THESE KIDS . . . CAME UP WITH ALL THEIR RULES AND STUFF.
NOW IT'S *MY* TURN.

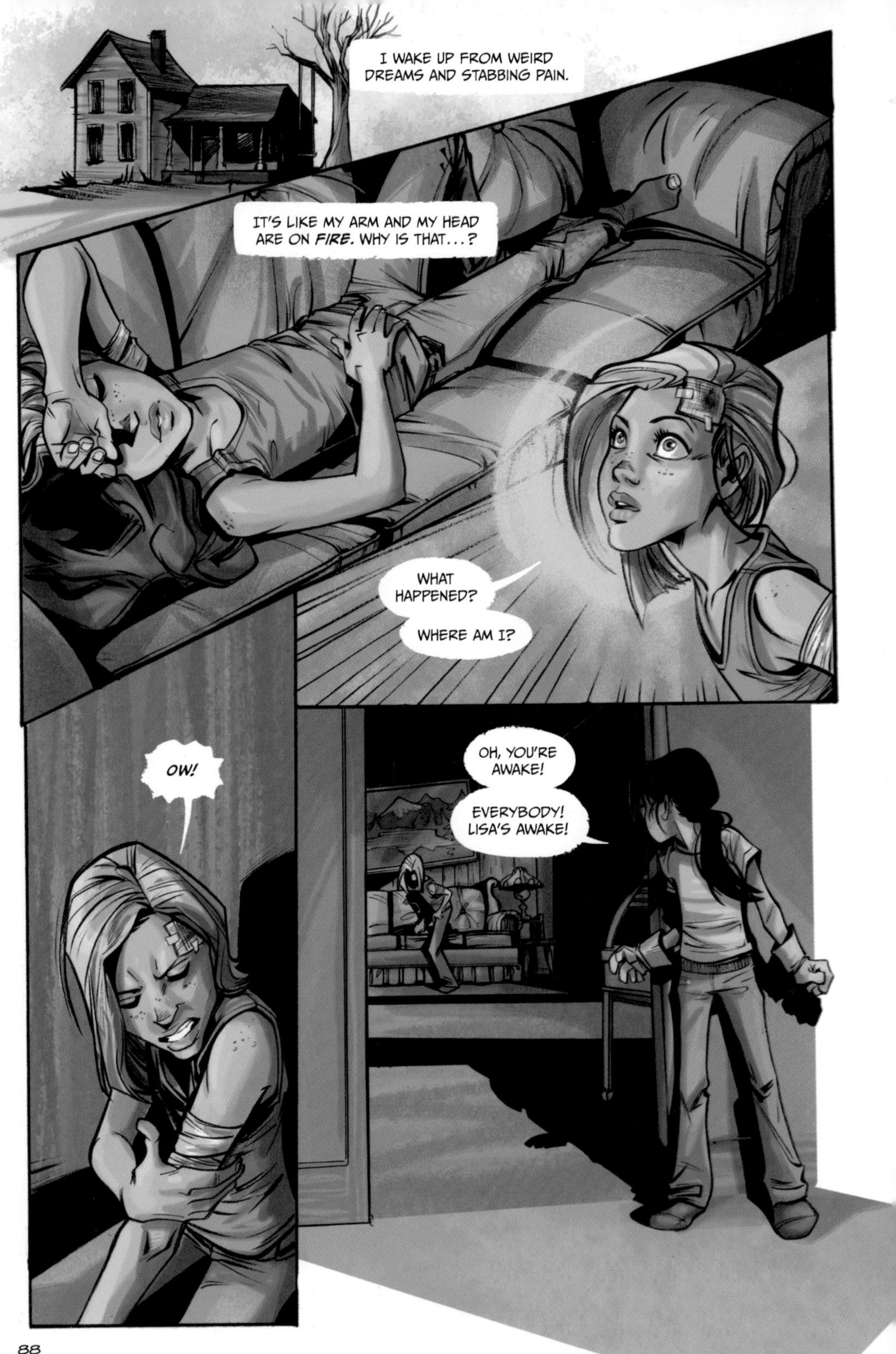
I WAKE UP FROM WEIRD DREAMS AND STABBING PAIN.
IT'S LIKE MY ARM AND MY HEAD ARE ON *FIRE.* WHY IS THAT...?
WHAT HAPPENED?
WHERE AM I?
OW!
OH, YOU'RE AWAKE!
EVERYBODY! LISA'S AWAKE!

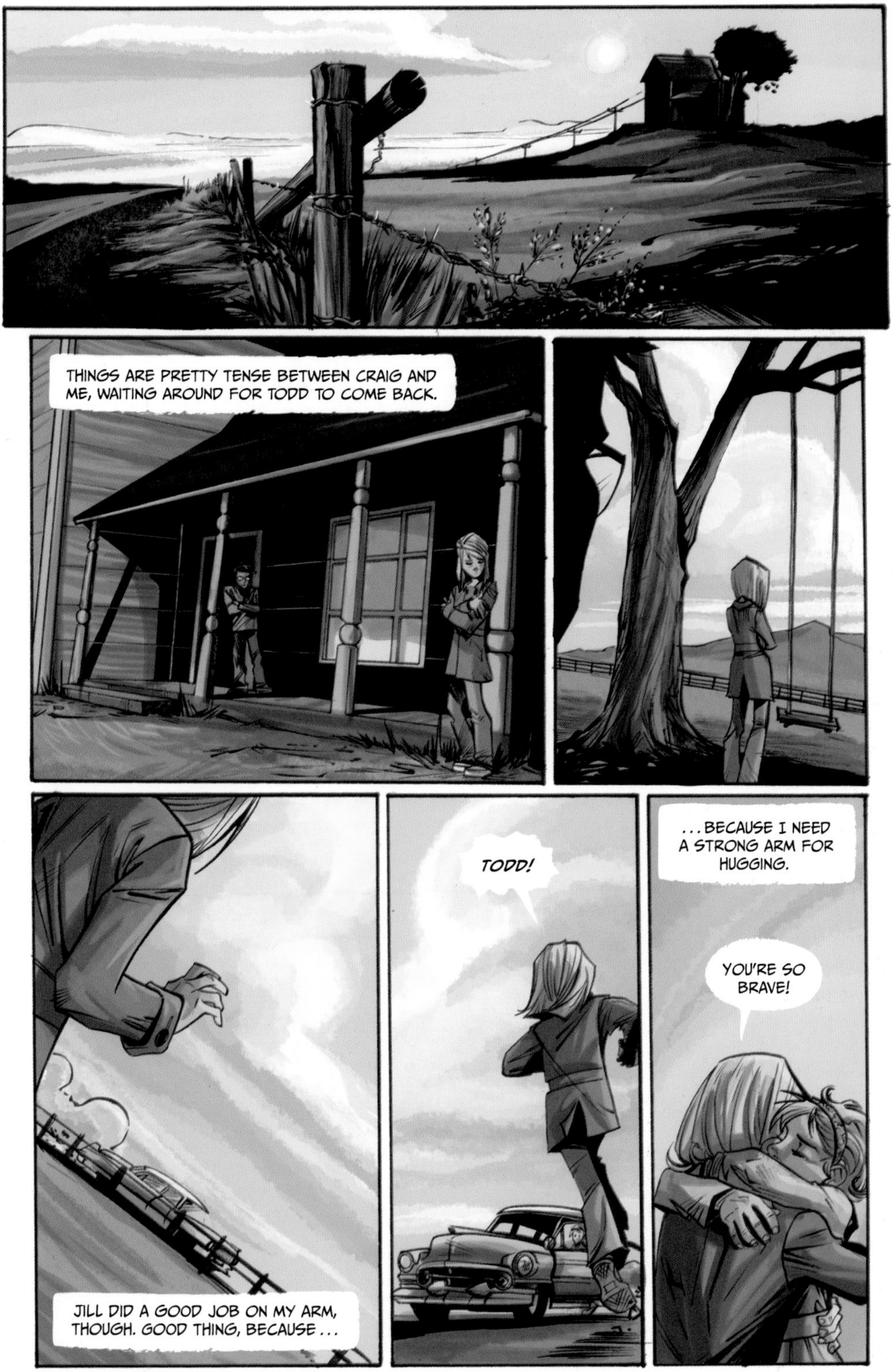
THINGS ARE PRETTY TENSE BETWEEN CRAIG AND ME, WAITING AROUND FOR TODD TO COME BACK.
JILL DID A GOOD JOB ON MY ARM, THOUGH. GOOD THING, BECAUSE . . .
TODD!
. . . BECAUSE I NEED A STRONG ARM FOR HUGGING.
YOU'RE SO BRAVE!

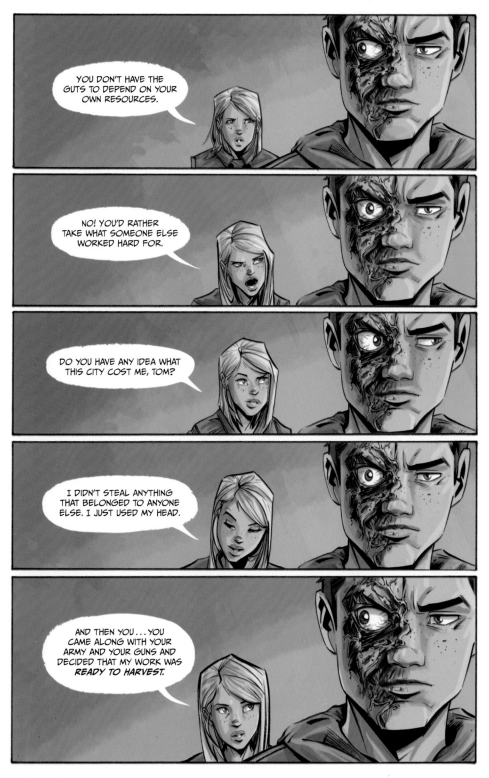